"How Well Do You Know Yourself, Chalis?" He Persisted.

"I've got better things to do than dwell on my own shortcomings!" Swinging her feet to the floor, she mumbled something about coffee, and Benjamin caught her wrist, tumbling her onto his lap.

"Don't evade the issue, Chalis. We both know perfectly well why you're running." His deep, slightly raspy drawl registered with telling results and then, before she could elude him, he turned her head and found her mouth.

In a single instant she was changed from a creature of reason into a mass of compelling needs. The only reality was Benjamin's arms holding her, his mouth moving sensitively over the contours of her lips as if he were memorizing her, intent on knowing every curve and secret place. . . .

DIXIE BROWNING

is a native of North Carolina, and many of her stories are born as she travels from her home in Winston-Salem to her cottage in Frisco, on Hatteras Island. She is also an accomplished watercolour artist, as well as a writer.

Dear Reader,

SILHOUETTE DESIRE is an exciting new line of contemporary romances from Silhouette Books. During the past year, many Silhouette readers have written in telling us what other types of stories they'd like to read from Silhouette, and we've kept these comments and suggestions in mind in developing SILHOUETTE DESIRE.

DESIREs feature all of the elements you like to see in a romance, plus a more sensual, provocative story. So if you want to experience all the excitement, passion and joy of falling in love, then SILHOUETTE DESIRE is for you.

I hope you enjoy this book and all the wonderful stories to come from SILHOUETTE DESIRE. I'd appreciate any thoughts you'd like to share with us on new SILHOUETTE DESIRE, and I invite you to write to us at the address below:

Jane Nicholls
Silhouette Books
PO Box 177
Dunton Green
Sevenoaks
Kent
TN13 2YE

DIXIE BROWNING

Shadow Of Yesterday

Published by Silhouette Books

First printing 1983

British Library C.I.P.

Browning, Dixie
Shadow of yesterday.—(Silhouette desire)
I. Title
813′.54[F] PS3552.R/

ISBN 0 340 34423 7

The characters and situations in this book are entirely imaginary and bear no relation to any real person or actual happening

Printed and bound in Great Britain for Hodder and Stoughton Paperbacks, a division of Hodder and Stoughton Ltd., Mill Road, Dunton Green, Sevenoaks, Kent (Editorial Office: 47 Bedford Square, London, WC1 3DP) by Richard Clay (The Chaucer Press) Ltd., Bungay, Suffolk

Other Silhouette Books by Dixie Browning

Unreasonable Summer
Tumbled Wall
Chance Tomorrow
Wren of Paradise
East of Today
Winter Blossom
Renegade Player
Island on the Hill
Logic of the Heart
Finders Keepers
Loving Rescue
A Secret Valentine
Practical Dreamer

1

Well, she'd see. See if two weeks of living without benefit of plumbing or electricity, without taxis and television, dinners at the Four Seasons and sales at Bloomingdales, without racing to a luncheon date, dashing to catch the phone, smiling and smiling until she thought her face would break—she'd see if she could survive without all that.

Bathing in the pond, lathering her hair as she stood in the clear, sweet water and then diving under its glassy surface as the suds streamed out behind her—that could scarcely be called a hardship. But the ants in her granola, the fast-melting ice in the insulated chest—those were things she could have done without.

At least they were problems she could come to grips with physically. Physically there was nothing wrong with her, other than being underweight. But emotionally she was a mess: a weepy, giddy-headed creature whose attention span had dwindled to zilch! Dress that up in a designer suit, paint a bright expression on its face and turn it loose on Manhattan Island, and you have a mobile disaster area!

This morning, a lone white heron had been her bathing companion. Stalking the perimeter of the six-acre pond, it had added to the feeling of dreamy unreality that had followed her south. Like the morning mist which was rising from the surface of the pond, it had been this same blasted mental fogginess, this inability to get through a single day lately without bursting into tears, that had sent her scurrying home in the first place.

God! She must have wept enough to float a battleship in the past few months. In the two days she had been here, she had cried over the lack of mirrors in the one-room cabin, over the wren's nest in the john, and over the fact that her only remaining relatives in the area were growing old. At least she had found one or two things to laugh about. Just lately, those had been scarce on the ground.

And she was so *tired!* But then, that was why she was here. She'd allowed two weeks to get herself sorted out. With militant precision, she'd staked out a schedule. She'd drain those tears out of her system this first week. After that she'd tackle the issues one at a time and deal with them as efficiently and effectively as she dealt with her job. If she could handle scheduling crises, fits of artistic temperament, clients whose credit ratings far outstripped their knowledge of art—not to mention reviewers who could annihilate years of work with a single misplaced adjective—then she could certainly cope with a minor case of mental fatigue.

Drifting aimlessly around the spring-fed pond on a yellow flowered air mattress, she laughed again, picturing Walt's face if he could see her now. For all she was probably going to marry him, Walter Gregory was definitely not a man for all seasons. He was purely a product of the City—capital C. Turned loose at a place like Quarter Moon Pond, he'd be at a dead loss.

To be fair, though, she had been just as much at a loss those first few months in New York. Freshly graduated from a small Southern college and brandishing a degree in art administration, she had tackled New York with an incredible amount of naïve optimism, thanks to having been nourished on the idea that she was the "talented" one of the family. Here in this particular pond, she had been a pretty fat frog, but in New York, she was just another tadpole, to be swallowed up if she didn't move fast enough.

Her feet struck the squishy bottom, stirring up a cloud of red mud, and she hurriedly hopped ashore, slicking excess water from her hair and the T-shirt she had slept in. She had bathed in it, washing both herself and the shirt, and she'd wear it until the sun dried it on her body. Her life was simplified, all right, and that, after all, had been the purpose of the whole back-to-nature exercise. Wasn't it Thomas Wolfe, a fellow Tarheel, who had said you can't go home again?

Well, she had. Under duress. Under Dr. Adelberg's warning that if she didn't slow up and take stock of who she was and where she was going, she'd end up weaving baskets in some secluded rural retreat.

Selecting a shiny green Granny Smith apple, she bit into it and stared out across the land where generations of Kenyons had raised corn, tobacco and more Kenyons. She'd come a long way from the skinny, saucer-eyed girl who used to fish this pond with a cane pole. She had grown up picnicking here with her parents, her grandparents, the aunts and uncles, and hoards of cousins. Quarter Moon had been the unofficial gathering place for the extended family.

For half of Davie County, as well. The Poe boys, Benjamin and Avery, for instance, had done their courting right here—a lot of it under the curious, if hidden, eyes of Chalis and her cousins. How often had they cut through the back pasture and come up through the woods to find one or both of the boys swimming with their girls? And not always with the benefit of bathing suits.

She had had a terrific crush on Benjamin back then. He had been eight or ten years older, an adult while she was still a child. Funny how she had forgotten all that. She had forgotten so much over six years, coming home only for her father's funeral, and then her grandfather's, and a month later, Gran Ada's. She had stayed three days after her father had died. Those other times, she had caught the next flight back. In the middle of divorcing Jorge, her mind had been stranded somewhere between New York and North Carolina.

No wonder she had forgotten the taste of pond water, the scent of honeysuckle and horsemint, the silky feel of red mud squishing between her toes. By the time she had made an appointment with Dr. Adelberg, she'd almost had to check her driver's license to be sure of her own name!

Rest. Time and rest and a complete lack of pressure, that had been the prescription; only how did one arrange it? How did one arrange an absence of pressure, knowing that as soon as the time was up, the same decisions were waiting to be made, decisions only she could make?

Two more days went by. Days in which Chalis fished with indifferent results, fried her catch over the one-eyed propane burner her Uncle Leonard had supplied, and listened to his and Aunt Steffie's friendly gossip on the afternoon they dropped by to check up on her.

"Mind you, honey, you're always welcome to come stay with us. I told Leonard that this place wasn't fit for pigs, much less a girl. It's grown up so much—seems like we never have time to come out here anymore."

"Back when you were a girl, Chalis, we used to keep a few head of cattle here to keep the grass down," Leonard declared.

Leonard and Stephany Kenyon drove off after reiterating their invitation to Chalis to come stay with them in Mocksville if she got tired of roughing it in the one-room cabin.

The sun went down, staining the air with a clear amethyst light as she continued to stare out over the pond. The discordant cry of a water turkey, the iridescent, snakelike anhinga, broke through her consciousness, and she realized that the muscles at the base of her neck were gathered into hard knots again. How many times had she roused herself from a trancelike state to find the muscles of her shoulders gathered into fists of tension?

She must have been existing on adrenaline for years! Craning her long, slender neck, she reached behind her to pinch and twist the tendons. At least after Dr. Adelberg's warning she had had sense enough to make a break. Quarter Moon Pond was the embodiment of all that was safe and secure and happy in her past, and she had homed in on it instinctively.

Funny. It hadn't occurred to her that life here had not been standing still during all the years she had been gone. While she had been evolving from an overconfident, underexperienced, small-town girl into a successful career woman with one marriage behind her and the possibility of another one staring her in the face, plus a totally unexpected, totally unwanted legacy waiting to be dealt with, the family that had once seemed so solid and everlasting had suddenly dissipated into thin air. Only Uncle Leonard and Aunt Steffie and their scattered offspring were left.

As the early June evening slowly cooled off, Chalis stood, stretched, and made her way to the cabin, automatically stomping to alert any snakes. The single room still held the warmth of the sun. It was comfortable enough, even though it was only sketchily furnished, with two bunks, a couple of straight chairs, and a picnic table and benches. There was a charcoal grill on the raised hearth—the rock fireplace had never drawn properly—and the windows on all sides looked out over the pond and the surrounding woods.

No wonder Uncle Leonard had hesitated to hand over his key. Even the old generator that used to provide power now housed a family of field mice. Instead, she made do with candles and lanterns and an insulated chest.

Still, it was precisely what she needed: a few concrete problems to sink her teeth into, problems she could solve with her own bare hands. A sort of latter-day Outward Bound experience. Maybe it would have the effect of sharpening her mind enough to decide what to do about Walt.

It had been through Walt that she had met Jorge. When the small SoHo gallery where she had worked on first coming to New York had folded, she had put on her one and only really good suit and her most comfortable pumps, tucked her résumé into her purse and started making the rounds. Corticelli's, on Madison Avenue, had just lost its bookkeeper, and while bookkeeping wasn't what she had come to New York for, it was a foot in the right door. With a year and a half's experience behind her and her degree in art administration, she had been hired.

Walt had since told her that he would have hired her if she'd had a degree in auto mechanics. He had been attracted to her looks, and had only later come to appreciate her very real skills. It had been those same looks that had made Jorge Joel Armister decide to add her to his collection: the cheekbones, the full lips, the short straight nose and the combination of silvery beige hair and large brown eyes—all accidents of nature for which she could claim no credit. Only she hadn't realized at the time, not until it was much too late, that it was only her shell Jorge wanted.

A late bloomer, she had been no match for the suave, devastatingly handsome man, whose sole interest in life was the collection of rare and beautiful things. He had likened her to the long-necked, sad-eyed women in his Modigliani paintings and had delighted in selecting pieces of his valuable collection of Victorian jewelry with which to ornament her for his friends' admiration.

Damn it, she refused to allow Jorge to intrude on her privacy! If the time ever came when she could think about her late ex-husband without threat of an ulcer, then that would be time enough to reevaluate the miserable experience and put it away for good.

Before turning in for the night, Chalis walked down to the gate to be sure her uncle had locked it behind him. She also locked her rental car. She had parked it behind a stand of pines; there was no point in advertising her presence in this isolated place. In years past there had been occasional trespassers, people who climbed the barbed wire fences to fish or swim. She could do without that sort of attention. Living in New York had taught her very quickly that one didn't take unnecessary risks.

It was impossible to know how long she had been asleep when she bolted up, her heart slamming at her throat, to hear the squeak of the door opening and then, almost instantly, a string of highly original profanity.

She had locked that door! She distinctly remembered doing it. Vainly trying to pierce the suffocating darkness, she was afraid to breathe, afraid to move a muscle.

Something crashed to the floor, and there came an almost simultaneous howl of pain. Chalis dropped an arm down beside the bunk to where she had left her flashlight, and her fingers struck it and sent it rolling.

Instant silence. Ringing, vacuumlike silence, when neither Chalis nor the intruder dared breathe. Then a harsh male voice cut through the atmosphere like a hot knife through butter. "Who the hell are you? What are you doing in here?"

Frantically she groped for the flashlight. It was the nearest thing to a weapon she had. Her fingers traced paths through the dust under the bunk, and she felt the cold metal just as a heavy weight pinned her by the shoulders to the hard mattress.

"All right, fellow, no tricks now," the man grated. "Just take it easy and nobody will get hurt."

Fellow! He thought she was a man? If only he could go on thinking that, she might come out of this encounter with nothing worse than bruised shoulders and heart failure.

"Speak up. What's going on here? Besides a spot of breaking and entering, that is."

"N-nothing," Chalis whispered hoarsely, making her voice as deep as she could. If she could only get rid of him before he got curious and lighted one of the candles. "My buddies and I—ah—were just frog gigging," she invented wildly. If he thought there were several of them, armed with needle-sharp gigs, then perhaps he wouldn't be so eager to hang around.

Something cold and wet dripped on her face, and she shuddered. Even the hands that gripped her shoulders felt cold and wet. All the horror stories she had ever heard converged in her mind, and she began to struggle, totally unaware of the whimpering sounds that came from between her frozen lips.

"What the hell—" The hands slipped down her arms, binding them to her sides. She kicked out frantically, only to have her legs anchored by a hard knee. "You just bought yourself a peck of trouble, boy. I'm sick and tired of you kids crashing here, littering up the place with beer cans and wine bottles!"

The wet leg was rough with hair on Chalis's soft, satiny skin, and she only hoped the man wasn't as aware of the texture of her body as she was of his. She could argue her rights some other time. For now, all she wanted to do was lock herself in her car and cover the seven miles to Uncle Leonard's house in record time. He had warned her of the occasional trespasser, but she had been so sure of her ability to look after herself.

Growling as harshly as she could, she wriggled away from those crippling hands. "I'm going, I'm going." Thank God it was as dark as the inside of midnight here in the cabin! If she could just lay hands on her purse, with her keys in it, the rest of her stuff could rot here!

She felt the heat of his body, and she quickly sidestepped, reaching out to the chair, where she thought she remembered leaving her bag. Instead, her hand came into contact with hard, cool flesh and she jumped back, striking the foot of one of the cross-legged benches with her bare toe.

The yelp of pain hadn't even left her throat before he had her pinned again, this time by the upper arms. She could actually feel his nearness, smell the clean, sweet scent of the pond water mingled with something musky and decidedly unsettling. "There's not much to you, is there, boy?" the intruder gritted, his voice slower, registering a note of curiosity. His hands slipped down her arms, the fingers ringing her slender bones easily. She had always been slender. For a while her leanness had been a fashionable asset. Now, after months of being unable to eat, unable to sleep, she had grown gaunt as a scarecrow.

She tried to wrench herself away, but he held her fast. "Oh, no. Let's have a little light on the subject and see just what manner of creature we've trapped here," he drawled.

"No!"

"No?" One of his hands left her arm, and she heard him fumbling with the things on the table. There had always been a tin can of kitchen matches there, as long as she could remember. It was still there after all these years, and the man obviously knew it.

"Please," she agonized. "I'll go peacefully. Only let me find my purse."

He leaped on the word before it was even out. "Purse?"

"My keys! Just let me—"

It was too late. She heard the plastic lid snap off

the old coffee can, and then the sulfury scent of a wooden match struck her nostrils as the light flared. The man nurtured the small blaze until he had located a candle, and then the small circle of yellowish light spread to reveal a gleaming wet male body—totally devoid of clothing.

Chalis turned away abruptly and dropped her face into her hands with a groan, but not before her mind had registered the threatening glower of black brows under a shock of unruly silver-streaked dark hair. There was a quick impression of strong, angular features, of tightly compressed lips and an endless expanse of hair-patterned chest before the candle flickered low, then flared up.

Her groan was smothered by his muttered oath, and then he was spinning her around to face him. Furious eyes blazed into hers as he held her away to examine her. They took in the deep hollows under her prominent cheekbones, the disarray of her shoulder-length hair, and then ranged down over her painfully lean body in the thin pink T-shirt and bikini panties she slept in.

"Who the hell are you?" A strange note had replaced the anger in his voice. Even in the semi-darkness she could feel his eyes on her, and a shiver of something atavistic seemed to hover in the air.

Chalis shook her head wordlessly. Curiously enough, she was no longer actually afraid, but she couldn't discount her precarious position. "Look," she managed finally, "I'm not hurting anything. I—I happen to be the owner of this property"—which was close enough to the truth—"so maybe you'd better—"

"The hell you are!"

Raw nerves snapped back instantly. "The hell I'm not! You're the intruder here!" She struggled to pull her arm from the steely manacle of his fingers. "This land has been in my family for generations, and if you don't leave this minute, I'll—"

"Who are you?" he rasped.

Her vision was becoming adjusted to the dim light now. She saw the blazing gleam of his eyes, and then it was lost as they narrowed to study her face minutely. Recognition came to her even as her stunned gaze fell from his face along the sinewy lines of his lean body, the broad chest with a pattern of hair that tapered down past a narrow waist. It was evidently mutual, for before she could voice her discovery, the man spoke. "You're—you've got to be one of the Kenyon kids. The skinny one. Carolyn? Charlotte?"

The laughter that bubbled from her lips was partly hysterical relief from tension, partly in remembrance of the last time she had seen this same man. Then, as now, he had been without benefit of clothing.

"I'd like to know just what the devil you find so funny," he snarled, and she doubled over, her arm slipping from his loosened grasp.

"It's you," she gasped. "You're Benjamin! I'd know you anywhere," she declared, and then howled again at the inadvertent implication.

Muttering something in exasperated tones, the tall man turned away and blew out the candle. "You haven't improved with age, have you?"

"N-not noticeably," she admitted, sobering now. A shuddering sigh left her, and she moved backward until she felt the edge of the bunk against her legs. She dropped down on it and said, "You are Benjamin Poe, aren't you?"

"I thought you said you'd know me anywhere?" His tone was slightly surly—not that Chalis could blame him. If he was recalling the many times long ago when a tall skinny tomboy with a cane pole had barged through the woods to find a teenaged Benjamin and his girl friend of the moment skinny-dipping in the pond, then it was no wonder he didn't remember her with any great degree of fondness.

"Have you got a towel around here?"

"Sure. Wait a minute, I'll find it for you." The laughter still trembled under her voice. Lately her emotions seemed to seesaw radically between tears and giggles, the one usually merging into the other.

"I'd appreciate it," Benjamin said with exaggerated politeness.

"Where are your clothes?"

"Outside on one of the benches. I thought I'd left a towel in here last summer."

"Your mouse built a nest in it. Here, be my guest." She handed him one of the two towels she had brought with her.

"Believe me, if I'd had any idea you were here," he observed dryly, "I'd have steered clear of the place."

Chalis could sense his movements as he dried himself off. She was enjoying herself now, cast back to a time when everything had been so much simpler. "You do realize, don't you, that I've seen you naked more times than I have clothed? You and

Avery used to go skinny-dipping here at least once a week, and not always alone."

"And you, of course, were always sneaking around in the bushes watching. We felt a certain obligation to keep you entertained, not to say educated. God, you must have been a precocious child!"

She blurted an instant denial. "I was not peeping! You were hardly hiding, anyway, and after all, it was Granddaddy's property. Besides, I was only a child."

There was a sound of movement, and then the bunk sagged beside her as he sat down. "All long legs, long neck and greedy eyes."

"Oh, thanks a lot! For your information, all I wanted to do was to catch that huge bass that kept breaking Daddy's line and stealing his plugs, but whenever we came down here, you and Avery and your girl friends had already settled in for the duration. I used to sneak through the woods and fish in the lower arm of the pond while you all cavorted on the other side of the point. Did you know how well the sound of voices travels on water?" she taunted.

"If we'd known you were there, we'd have given a better performance."

"You did well enough, thanks. Believe me, I learned more from you that last summer than I ever did in school."

She could feel his vital presence in the small room and she edged further toward the end of the bunk, curling her legs up beside her. Benjamin Poe. Lord, she had had a king-sized crush on him back in those days! Funny, she hadn't thought of him in ages, and now it seemed as if New York and the intervening years had never happened. "Tell me, Benjamin, what are you doing now, still farming?"

"Still farming," he affirmed. "I moved into Granddad's place, Yadkin Trace, several years ago. Like yours, my family has dwindled over the years. Avery and I are the last, and when he wanted out of the cow business, I bought him out. He's living in Atlanta now, running a chain of restaurants."

"And you?" she persisted.

"Oh, I managed to pick up a degree or two in between milking and feeding up. We dispersed the dairy herd a few years back and put in beef. But what about you? I seem to recall hearing you'd gone to art school."

"I wanted to, but when I discovered I wasn't quite the paragon my parents thought I was, I settled for art administration. After that, I went to New York."

He moved slightly and his thigh brushed against Chalis's knee, causing her to flinch away instinctively. She studiously avoided looking at him, feeling oddly self-conscious. It's only Benjamin, she reasoned to herself unsuccessfully. Reason had been her short suit just lately.

"So now you're a city girl, administering art, whatever that entails. So what the dickens are you doing camping out here at Quarter Moon? And incidentally, which Kenyon are you? One of Leonard's?"

"I'm Chalis, Edward and Lorie's only contribution to the clan." She shot him a glance, noticing the cut of his hard cheekbones and the strength of his proud nose in the faint starlight coming through the windows. As his own speculative gaze tangled with hers, she dropped her eyes quickly. "As to my job, I started out keeping books for a small gallery in SoHo, and I'm now the assistant to the director of a Madison Avenue gallery. Not the assistant director, mind you—there's a subtle difference. Actually, it's a fancy title for a Jill-of-all-jobs, and pressure goes with the territory. I needed a break, so . . ."

"So you came home," he finished.

"Home is an apartment in New York, now," she corrected dryly.

"I'm surprised Leonard would allow you to stay here alone. Trespassers are still a problem, not to mention snakes, now that the place has been allowed to grow up."

"It's fine the way it is. I'm not afraid of varmints, either the two-legged or the no-legged variety, and I enjoy roughing it occasionally." She didn't bother to add that copperheads and itinerant fishermen were a lot easier to deal with than the subtle pressures of an unwanted legacy, a persistent suitor and the not-so-subtle pressures of her demanding job.

"A pretty bold statement, even for an assistant-to-the-director who's a Jill-of-all-jobs, Miss Kenyon . . . or is it Mrs. now? At any rate, I tip my hat to you."

"It's Ms.," she retorted astringently, and then, with a rise of humor, added "and under the circumstances, you're in no position to tip your hat to anyone, Mr. Poe."

"Under the circumstances, I believe you're right," he agreed readily, and she could tell he was smiling from the tone of his voice. The voice was deeper now than it had been all those years ago—slower, with a thoughtful note that managed to infiltrate with disconcerting ease the barriers she had erected over the years.

They both fell silent. Oddly enough, Chalis was totally unembarrassed by Benjamin's nudity; she felt almost completely relaxed here in the sheltering darkness. It held all the impersonal safety of a confessional.

"How long do you plan on staying?" he asked after a while.

"Two weeks from last Monday. Uncle Leonard told me no one ever used the place anymore."

"Your uncle's never around when I stop off for a late-night swim."

Uncurling one leg to relieve the pins and needles in it, she asked, "Do you do it often?"

He stood up then. She was as aware of his movements as if her eyes could cut through the darkness. "Fairly," he admitted. "It's a convenient stop-off between Dutchman's Creek and Yadkin Trace, and we've been weighing and tagging calves at the creek all day. Dusty as hell! Next to a cold beer, a quick dip was about the most refreshing thing I could think of." He grinned, and she caught the flash of strong white teeth. "Sure you won't change your mind about roughing it out here? You're most welcome to come home with me."

"Thanks, Benjamin, but this place is exactly what I need at the moment."

"You're the doctor." He had moved over toward the screened door, and she could barely see him silhouetted against the starlit sky. She had forgotten the breadth of his shoulders, the lean taper of his flanks. He was taller than she remembered, too—several inches taller than her own five feet eight. His arms and shoulders showed the results of years of hard manual labor on the farm. A degree in agriculture or animal husbandry or whatever still didn't preclude long days of hard physical labor, with little time left over for anything else.

Stirring herself, she rose to see him off. "It was good seeing you again, Benjamin," she murmured, immediately wincing at her inadvertent double entendre. She heard his soft laugh, and her own reluctant one mingled companionably with it for a moment.

Benjamin Poe. After all these years, she mused, lying on her back in the darkness. Her first big heartthrob. Her first anatomy lesson, as well, she recalled with a slow grin of amusement. She'd been about fourteen the last time she had seen him. Benjamin had been in his first year of college, home for a weekend, looking mature and broodingly handsome to her impressionable eyes.

She'd soon forgotten him in the rush of getting through high school, throwing herself into studio art classes at college and then slogging away at the less exciting administrative end of the business.

Benjamin! Lord, he had figured in more than one of her daydreams all those years ago. That lean face with the expressive mouth and the intense, deep-set eyes. He had had more girls crazy for him than any boy she knew, and if he had seemed to pay her the slightest bit more notice than he did the rest of the noisy young Kenyons, she had long since chalked it up to her overactive, adolescent imagination. Somewhere along the way, she had lost her romantic illusions. There had been several boy friends along the way, and then Jorge had come along like an unbelievably suave Prince Charming. He had courted her expertly, never once pressuring her where sexual matters were concerned, and she had appreciated his consideration in "waiting for marriage."

Unfortunately, it hadn't been worth waiting for, only how could she have known that? The lack had been on both sides: Jorge wasn't particularly interested, and, after a while, she wasn't, either.

Restlessly, she turned onto her side and concentrated on sleep. There was no point in dwelling on the past—nor on the unsettling effect of finding a nude male in one's boudoir in the middle of the night. She'd leave that sort of thing to those who needed something to add zest to their life.

What was that old fractured maxim of her grandfather's? You buttered your bread . . . now lie in it!

2

Awakening to the sun-dappled reflection of the pond dancing across the ceiling, Chalis breakfasted on fruit and instant coffee. She had picked up the necessary items to make use of the charcoal grill and a fresh bottle of propane for the one-eyed ring that heated water at the store the day before. All in all, she was finding immense satisfaction in being able to fall back on her own resources after years of city living.

Last night had been . . . interesting. Granted, she had come here to get away from people, but all the same, it was hard to quit cold turkey. Maybe an occasional bit of relaxed conversation with an old hometown friend, someone totally unrelated to her present situation, would be just the ticket. Of course, Benjamin was hardly a friend. They were separated by less than ten years, but at the time when she had known him, he had been an adult, and she a child.

Standing at the edge of the water in her nylon briefs and T-shirt, she reinflated the leaky air mattress and launched herself out onto the pond. She didn't own a bathing suit—had hardly needed one in all the years she had been in New York. Jorge had considered swimming a primitive pastime at best, and she suspected Walt held more or less the same view.

She had worked for Walt Gregory for just four months and had dated him several times when he had introduced her to one of his best clients, Jorge J. Armister. Almost immediately, Jorge had launched an intensive campaign, directing all his considerable ammunition against her comparative lack of experience. She had been mesmerized, captivated, stunned that a man of Jorge's caliber could fall in love with a gawky girl from Smith Grove.

It had been natural for Chalis to go to Walt when she had escaped from her disastrous marriage. At the risk of losing a valuable client, he had hired her again. She had been, and still was, overwhelmingly grateful.

She had quickly moved ahead as his assistant—and not just because of her administrative ability. She had learned a lot from Jorge—about people as well as art. He had taught her to dress up to her own unique style, to use makeup effectively to enhance the slender oval of her face, her large, long-lashed dark eyes and her full lips. He had cultivated her already sound instincts where art was concerned. He had also, over a period of slow disenchantment, taught her that her instincts as far as men were concerned were definitely not to be trusted.

Once they had been married, it had not taken her long to realize that her husband was incapable of so human an emotion as love. The nearest he came to love was what he felt for his collections of art and Victorian jewelry. They were something for Jorge to own and for other men to covet. And Chalis was a part of that collection.

By afternoon she was sleepy again. It would have been all too easy to go back to sleep. Instead, Chalis forced herself to unchain the battered old skiff that had been in use since her childhood. Devoid now of all but a few flakes of white paint, it nevertheless rode lightly across the pond as she straddled the bow cap and propelled herself stern first with the single paddle. A smile of pleased surprise lightened her features at the realization that she hadn't lost the knack of steering with a flick of the blade and a subtle shift of her weight.

So many things were coming back to her. It was as if she'd been asleep for a long time. "A blooming Snow White," she muttered, driving the stern up on the bank with a ferocious burst of paddling. "Deliver me from another handsome prince!"

There had been a pawpaw tree over in this corner, and down at the base of the spillway there had been passion vines climbing the barbed wire fence. Chalis was considering the wisdom of braving the tangle of blackberries, wild roses, honeysuckle and hundreds of young sycamores when someone hailed her from the other side of the pond.

"Hi! Chalis! Are you over there?"

It was Benjamin. Only now did she acknowledge to herself that his image, his essence, had ghosted her thoughts all morning. Hardly surprising, she rationalized, since he was the only person she had seen in days. "I'm over here on the dam. Why?"

"Where's your Southern hospitality, Miss Kenyon? How about picking me up?"

Perversely, she hesitated. "You could walk around," she parried.

"And run the gamut of ticks, snakes and chiggers? Look, if you insist, I'll swim, but I warn you, I didn't come prepared." His hand went to the belt buckle that glinted low on his hard, flat abdomen, and Chalis made a laughing dive for the skiff.

"Okay, okay, keep your pants on!"

She was a third of the way across, trying vainly to ignore the tall figure in jeans and faded chambray shirt who waited on the bank, when he called out, "Did you know that the bow of a boat is generally considered to be the front? Who taught you your seamanship?" He grasped the transom to steady the small wooden boat and, in one lithe motion, launched it again as he swung himself aboard.

"Granddaddy," Chalis replied. She deftly turned them with a sweeping pull of the paddle, endeavoring to conceal her delight in his company under a veneer of cool indifference.

"Did the old man also teach you to ride a horse?"

The indifference wavered, fractured, and fled at

the comparative mental image, and Chalis's reluctant giggle became a full-fledged laugh. Benjamin joined her as he leaned back, elbows braced on the transom and long legs stretched out toward her. Suddenly realizing where her gaze had settled, Chalis wrenched her eyes away and paddled furiously to the middle of the pond.

Forcing herself to assume a mantle of nonchalance, she said, "Did you have a specific address in mind, sir, or shall I just take a couple of turns around the park?"

His eyes crinkled in a lazy, taunting grin. "If I'd brought my fly rod you could have paddled me along the dam while I placed a few flies up under those alders."

"Dream on! I suppose you've trained all your early mermaids to paddle for you while you fish, haven't you? Do their services include dressing the catch and cooking it, too?"

"You'd be amazed at what their services include." The grin broadened wickedly. "Or maybe you wouldn't, at that."

While she searched for a suitable rejoinder, Benjamin's eyes roved over her, lingering appreciatively on the yellow tank top she wore with a pair of brief white terrycloth shorts before moving on to the lower arm of the crescent-shaped pond. "I wonder—did you ever explore the honeysuckle bottom when you were young?"

Following his gaze to the vine-covered gully, from which a shallow creek fed into the pond, she decided to pass on his oblique reference to her age. "No, not really. We turned the cows in there once or twice in a drought when the grass dried up, but as far as I know there's nothing there."

"Go ashore over there"—he pointed to a shelving section of the bank—"and come with me. If it's not too grown up, I'll show you something worth seeing."

Chalis followed Benjamin to where a remnant of barbed wire fence barred the way. "Under, over or through?" he asked, testing the flexibility of the top strand.

Gauging the height dubiously, Chalis opted for through. Benjamin placed a worn Western boot on the bottom strand and held the top one to its limit, and she angled one foot and leg gingerly through the gap. "This is ludicrous," she muttered, swinging her body sideways. Halfway under, she was on a level with Benjamin's tautly muscled thighs, and her peripheral vision brought a flare of inexplicable color to her face.

Emerging unharmed on the other side, she watched while he held down the top strand and swung one long, powerfully muscled leg over to the other side. He took the fence as if he were mounting a horse, and, midstride, he pretended to stumble, reaching out to catch Chalis's shoulder. His cool, hard hand seemed to burn her bare skin, and, flinching, she braced herself against his considerable weight. "Who taught you to climb a fence?" she taunted, forcing derision to her voice.

"Don't be impertinent, girl, or I won't show you the buzzard's nest," he threatened, shaking her with mock ferocity.

"*Buzzard's* nest. Are you serious?" She had paddled blisters onto her hands, waded through weeds and climbed a rusty old fence to look at a buzzard's nest?

"Ah, there speaks the jaded sophisticate. You're just out of touch with the simple pleasures of this world, honey. What you're about to see—I hope—is better than most of what you buy a ticket to see in the big city. Where do you think all those exotic animals in your zoos come from? Macy's basement?"

"This had better be good, Poe," Chalis muttered, wiping perspiration from her forehead as she followed his broad back along an all but obliterated path.

They reached a spot where a canopy of vines covered two enormous fallen trees, and Benjamin stayed her with a flat, calloused palm. "I'd better go first and be sure mama's not at home. I thought I saw her take off while we were out on the pond."

"What about snakes?"

"What about 'em? Stay close behind me and you'll be all right. There's a six-foot king snake who keeps the area safe for us mortals."

From her childhood Chalis had been taught that a king snake would devour other types, including the deadly copperhead. If there was a six-foot specimen in residence, then she supposed she should feel safe. All the same, she moved closer to Benjamin's crouching form as they entered the shadowy green tunnel formed by honeysuckle and muscadine vines over leaning and fallen trees.

They had gone perhaps five feet when he halted suddenly, causing her to cannon into his backside.

"You might have signaled," she whispered tersely, jumping back as her hand touched his lean, narrow buttock.

"Sorry." He reached around and caught her wrist, pulling her alongside him. She caught the faint scent of perspiration and cattle and some wildly stimulating aftershave, and it sent her pulses careening in a totally uncharacteristic manner. She swallowed convulsively and told herself not to be such an idiot.

Pointing to a small patch of sunlight that filtered through the honeysuckle, Benjamin turned a triumphant smile on her. "See? What did I tell you?"

They were snow white. There were two of them, huddled in the midst of an untidy wad of sticks and grasses, and, except for the unblinking black eyes and the grotesque yellow bills that seemed far too heavy for the slender little necks to support, they looked like the clusters of pale maribou that trimmed a pair of satin mules she had left behind in her apartment. "I don't believe it," she whispered. "Are they really buzzards?"

"Vultures—buzzard hawks. Part of Mother Nature's sanitation corps. Now tell me that they wouldn't rate a few oohs and ahhs in Central Park Zoo."

Emerging into the sunlight a few minutes later, Chalis shook her head slowly. "I can't believe it."

"You mean that something so attractive and helpless can grow up to be a hunter and a carrion seeker? A lot of creatures change in outward appearance as they grow older, Chalis, but that doesn't alter their basic nature." He led the way to the fence and paused for her to catch up.

"That's not what I meant." Already the image of the baby buzzards was fading, though, to be replaced by a much more powerful presence. Chalis considered her own uncharacteristic reactions with mild interest. It must be a holdover from years past, when just the thought that Benjamin might be here was enough to send her adolescent pulses galloping at an embarrassing rate.

He swung easily over the fence and spread the strands apart for her, and she grimaced, uncomfortably aware of his eyes on her backside as she maneuvered herself awkwardly into the gap. Her shirttail had parted company with her shorts, and she could see the fine film of perspiration gleaming on her thighs as she bent double and began to edge under.

Her luck deserted her. It was her hair that caught in one of the wicked barbs, and she hovered there, halfway through the fence, with one hand grabbing ineffectually at the tangled strands. "Help me, dammit!"

"Then be still." She could feel the warmth of his body enveloping her even before he touched her. "Here, lean against my leg."

She had no choice but to obey. Her muscles were already protesting the strain of her position, and she swore softly under her breath as she let her weight rest on Benjamin's thigh. His muscles felt like granite under her cheek—warm, vital granite. She was overpoweringly conscious of the scent of him again, adding the hint of laundry soap to the other strangely stimulating ingredients. Hardly understanding her reaction, she grew impatient to be free.

"Hold still," he snarled, his hand clasping her head as he worked to release her hair.

She clutched his knee as she swayed dizzily. Lord, of all the undignified positions to be caught in! "Just jerk it free," she growled. "I can spare it!"

"Wouldn't think of it," he muttered. His fingers seemed to be spending an inordinate length of time on her neck. "I've almost got it now. . . . It's like trying to untangle a cobweb. You in a bind?" he asked, as if suddenly realizing she might be cramped.

"Oh, of course not. I always relax like this. Just hurry up, will you?"

His hand cupped her head and then slid down to her shoulders, and he urged her through the fence. "All done, honey, and the patient lives to tell the tale." She staggered as she regained her balance, and he caught her to his side, swatting her bottom with a familiarity that had her hackles up before she could even pull herself from his arms.

"What's the matter? Are you upset because you're too stiff to climb a fence without coming to grief?" he asked with highly suspect innocence.

"Look who's talking," she jeered. "At least I didn't almost trip over the fence post!"

"Touché. Let's face it, honey, we're both over the hill. Maybe before you go back I'll challenge you to a rocking chair race. First one who falls over the edge of the porch loses."

He waited for her to reach the bow before shoving off and swinging himself onto the stern thwart. He could as easily have walked the few hundred feet to where his truck waited.

"You know, I was just thinking," Chalis mused, laying the dripping paddle across her knees as they drifted along the overgrown shoreline to the mooring post. "This time last week I was lunching at Four Seasons with my boss and the owner of a Tulsa department store while we did our best to convince him that his investment portfolio should be expanded to include original art. If anyone had told me that today I'd be crawling under barbed wire fences in search of buzzard's nests, I'd have called the butterfly squad."

Benjamin examined his nails with a comically smug expression. "It's just goes to show you, my dear, that there's hope for even the most underprivileged among us."

She swung the paddle, showering him with the few remaining drops of water, and then busied herself in making a perfect landing. "Did anyone ever tell you that the hay in your loft has spoiled?"

"Numerous times, but seldom in such poetic terms." He held the boat while she skipped agilely ashore, and swung into step with her as she headed for the cabin and a tall glass of cold water. Pouring two, she handed him one. "It's not icy, but it's still cold."

"It's fine," he assured her, throwing back his head to drain the plastic tumbler. Chalis watched in fascination as the muscles of his throat worked smoothly under the deeply tanned skin. She was still watching when he lowered his head and held out the tumbler to her, and she looked away in confusion after seeing the speculative glint in his eyes.

"Have you had lunch?" he asked her.

She nodded. "Raw peanuts, apples and a pickled egg."

He grimaced. "No wonder you're still a ninety-seven-pound weakling. What about dinner?"

"Not yet! I realize there's a difference in country and city dinner hours, but it's just after two o'clock."

"I meant, what about having dinner . . . with me. We could compromise on the hour if you'll forgive a few grumblings of an unsophisticated stomach."

Disappointment all out of proportion swept over her as she said, "Oh, Benjamin, I'm sorry. I promised Aunt Steffie I'd have dinner with them. She's fixing chicken and dumplings especially for me, and she'll already have put her hen on to stew by now." Her lashes swept down over her expressive eyes, and she missed the look that flashed across his face. When he spoke, however, his voice was carefully casual.

"No problem, honey. Just thought I'd offer."

Not *ask*, she noted, but *offer*. As if he were doing her a favor. Who knows, she mused wryly, maybe he was.

She watched him saunter out to where his silver pickup truck was parked in the shade of a small grove of persimmon trees, unconsciously admiring the gracefulness of his long-legged stride.

When he tossed a casual salute over his shoulder and called back, "Thanks for the boat ride, Chalis. Give your folks my regards," she thought, good Lord, girl, you're worse off than we thought! Voyeurism, yet!

By the time the engine sounds had faded, she was

still standing there, bemused by a flock of half-formed thoughts and ideas. Shaking her head impatiently, she pushed aside her disappointment. She was looking forward to visiting with her aunt and uncle again, and after all, she didn't even know Benjamin—not really. Nor was there any future in cultivating the slight acquaintance, since she'd be leaving in little over a week. He was likable enough. Physically he was one of the most attractive men she had seen in a long time, but the last thing she needed now was to reactivate her old adolescent crush on the farmer next door!

3

Chalis's evening with her aunt and uncle had been good for her. Steffie's country cooking was a fine art, and the unpretentious warmth of their home in Mocksville was the best medicine she could think of for what ailed her. All the same, her thoughts had strayed to Benjamin several times while Leonard rambled on about taxes and someone's Charolais bull, which had got loose and was finally rounded up on the courthouse square. What would dinner with Benjamin have been like? Where would he have taken her?

She fell asleep that night smiling at an image of Benjamin as he lay sprawled out in the stern of the skiff. Tossing restlessly, she dreamed of king snakes and Jorge and maribou slippers and a young Benjamin lining up a row of bathing beauties in rocking chairs. She awakened reluctantly, conscious of the gathering heat in the small cabin. Barely seven and already a scorcher. It was too hot to go back to sleep, at any rate.

Chalis had slept a good deal lately—part of an escape mechanism, according to Dr. Adelberg, the analyst she had started seeing when she had unaccountably found herself weeping bucketfuls for no good reason at all. At least that malady seemed to be on the way out.

She got thought a lazy day with scarcely a depressing thought, fishing with little luck and swimming laps across the pond with dogged persistence. She was struggling to light the grill in order to cook the one small fish she had caught when she heard someone approaching on the graveled driveway that wound through the woods to the clearing around the cabin.

Looking up, she saw Benjamin swing out of the high cab of his pickup truck and wave cheerfully. "Caught 'em all yet?"

"Caught 'em all what?" she demanded exasperatedly. "You're just in time to get this blasted thing going for me."

He accomplished the deed with an efficiency that put her to shame. "What are you planning to cook, steak?"

"Nothing so mundane," she replied airily, unwrapping the four-inch bream she had taken on the spinning rod she had borrowed from her uncle.

"I can see that if I want to eat, I'd better get busy. No wonder you're still so skinny." His eyes moved over her slender body; the swell of her small, ripe breasts was clearly revealed in the pink T-shirt she wore with a pair of lurid Hawaiian print trunks she had found hanging on a nail behind the door.

"The term is slender," she informed him in her haughtiest manner. She struck a model's pose, her eyes sparkling with pleasure at seeing him again.

"Semantics," he growled, circling her waist with his long, capable hands. "You wouldn't make a ripple if I threw you overboard."

Her fists went to his shoulders as she laughingly pushed him away, fighting the odd, choking sensation that seemed to afflict her whenever he touched her. "I seem to remember that you always did like your women pretty well rounded," she said a little breathlessly. "What ever happened to that bosomy little brunette who used to squeal 'Oh, *Benji*' all the time?"

"I married her."

Chalis's arms dropped limply to her side and she grimaced, gazing apologetically into Benjamin's deep-set hazel eyes. "Oh, Lord, me and my hoof-and-mouth disease!"

"Forget it. Now, if I'm going to catch my supper, I'd better get busy. I'd say a small popping bug ought to be about right this time of day, wouldn't you?"

Chalis wiped the film of pollen off the outdoor table and got out paper plates, napkins and plastic cutlery. She hated drinking wine from plastic cups, but it was the best she could do under the circumstances. While the coals burned down to a pale glow, she wandered down to where Benjamin was fly-fishing, to discover he had already caught three bass in the twelve-inch range.

"Won't your wife be expecting you?"

"Jean and I were divorced several years ago." Whipping the tapered line out from the end of the split bamboo rod, he placed the tiny lure up under an overhanging branch and twitched it gently. Instantly, the surface of the water erupted, and then the battle was on. Chalis sat on the ground and watched entranced as Benjamin manipulated a whopping granddaddy of a largemouth bass, using patience, cunning and skill. At times she thought surely the slender, whiplike rod would break under the furious assault, but finally Benjamin managed to net the spent fish and remove the lure from his bony lip.

"Good fight, old fellow. You've earned a reprieve." He tossed him back, and Chalis tilted her head in puzzlement.

"After all that trouble to catch him, you throw him back?"

He unhooked a stringer and shouldered his rod. "The fun's in the angling. I enjoy trying my hand at outwitting a fish by offering him what he wants, where and when he wants it, without spooking him in the process. As for keeping him"—he shrugged his wide shoulders—"I've always thrown back those I don't need . . . or want." He cast her an enigmatic look from under the shelf of his brows, and Chalis forced herself to dismiss the odd impression that they weren't discussing fish.

The moment passed. He held up the string of smaller bass and grinned at her, and Chalis was struck again by the knowledge that Benjamin Poe was even more attractive than he had been all those years ago. His hair was still as thick, although the mahogany was laced with gray now, so that it contrasted strikingly with his perennial tan. His nose was as proud, his full bottom lip beneath the sterner top one as sensual as it had been back in the days when she used to watch him with his girl friends and then go home and dream about him.

"And you didn't remarry?" The words were an unconscious extension of her thoughts, and she winced at her own lack of tact. She didn't usually blunder socially, but oddly enough, the idea of Benjamin's being married stuck like a burr in her mind.

"Nope. I always try to learn from my mistakes. From that particular one I learned that my judgment in women isn't very good. Since then, I've kept things on pretty much a casual basis." He slung his catch onto the board nailed to a pine tree and reached for the cleaning tools. "What about you? No husband yet? I'd have thought you'd be only too eager to sample all those forbidden delights you used to sneak about trying to catch a glimpse of. Not," he added dryly, "that marriage is a prerequisite these days."

She dropped down onto the bow of the nearby skiff to watch him clean the fish, absently stroking the satiny skin of the leg she propped up on the gunnel. "I didn't sneak about, and if it's any comfort to you, I didn't actually see any of what you call forbidden delights!"

He tossed a grin over his shoulders and she almost missed it. Her eyes were on his hands. They were strong hands—long, beautifully formed and surprisingly well kept for a farmer.

"I'd be glad to arrange for a personal demonstration," he bantered, laying aside a fat roe.

"No thanks," she retorted repressively. "I'm far more interested in dinner." Surprisingly enough, she was. Her appetite, at least, was improving, even if her mind was as hopelessly fogged in as ever. And even when the fog lifted, she seemed to be plagued with all sorts of unlikely notions.

"You don't know what you're missing," he gibed.

"I'll take your word for it." Her stomach growled, and he laughed, breaking the small frisson of tension that had shivered between them for an instant.

The fish were delicious. As darkness fell, they drank the unchilled wine and ate with their fingers, laughing as the delicious juices dripped down their arms. Chalis sighed, licking off her sticky fingers as hoards of insects and frogs tuned up in a deafening chorus. "And I thought New York was noisy!"

"There are noises, and then there are noises."

"And you prefer country noises," she prompted.

"Don't you?"

The chorus cut off as abruptly as it had begun, and they listened almost breathlessly until a single bullfrog resumed his *bay-rum* chant. "I'd better not," she murmured dryly. "My job's waiting for me back in New York."

Moving with the quiet efficiency she was already coming to recognize as characteristic of him, Benjamin stood and gathered the litter of disposable dishes and carried them to the trash. "Come on—washup time," he called softly.

"Wash *what?*" There weren't even any pans to wash.

"Wash *us*," he announced, the words muffled as he pulled his shirt off over his head.

"You can't be serious!"

"What did you plan to do, stir up the mud at the edge of the pond trying to dip and dab? Come on, shed your inhibitions and dive in. Unless you'd rather lurk in the bushes and watch me again?"

"You wretch!" She swung a leg over the bench and stood up. Benjamin was already shedding his trousers, and this time, she saw with relief, he wore a pair of dark, extremely brief trunks. "I don't have a bathing suit," she parried.

"When have you ever known me to object to that?"

"The circumstances are slightly different," she reminded him tartly.

"Are they?" His voice was suspiciously bland, and she hesitated at the edge of the water, uncomfortably conscious of the stickiness of her hands and the silent invitation of the warm, star-sprinkled waters.

Benjamin's lean body sliced the surface with scarcely a splash; but still she lingered, increasingly aware of a feeling of subliminal excitement, as if she were back in her early teens, watching him while she pretended to fish.

"Do I have to toss you in?" he challenged. His face was a pale blur as he trod water a dozen yards out from shore.

"It's dangerous to swim after eating."

"It's dangerous to stand there daring me to come after you," he rejoined softly.

She waded out and then launched herself face down. The water was silky and sweet, considerably warmer than the night air, and she rolled over onto her back and floated out toward the center of the pond. There were snapping turtles and water snakes sharing it with her, but logic told her they were far more frightened of her than she of them. Her shivering awareness was of another sort, and she was oddly fascinated by her own reactions. She hadn't wanted a man for a long, long time. She certainly didn't want Benjamin—not *that* way. The movement of her arms grew more agitated, and she made a conscious effort to contain her restlessness.

"Slow down, water witch," came the deep, unexpected drawl behind her, and she tipped her head backward and floundered, submerging awkwardly. She surfaced almost immediately with Benjamin's hands holding her upright. His hard fingers bit into her rib cage, and he laughed, his breath warm against the dampness of her face. "I should have known you didn't have much built-in flotation. Maybe this wasn't such a brilliant idea, after all."

"I'm all right," she gasped. "You just startled me, that's all." Her legs were churning faster than necessary, and she could feel the pulse beating just below her ears. When her legs tangled with his, she floundered, trying frantically to disengage herself.

"What ails you, Chalis? You can swim, can't you? I thought you Kenyons were like a school of guppies when it came to the water."

"Of course I can swim," she snapped indignantly, only the words came out sounding more breathless than anything else, and he laughed then, a sound that triggered a peculiar reaction along her spine.

"Then what's wrong? Are you afraid I might revert to type and do—this?"

Before she could avoid him, he pulled her against him, finding her mouth with unerring accuracy in the dim brilliance of the starlight. The sweet taste of pond water was on her tongue, the feel of his full bottom lip surprisingly firm against her startled mouth.

Chalis struggled and then felt the water closing over her head. Benjamin did not relinquish his hold, nor did his mouth break contact with hers. As he kicked them to the surface again, with Chalis's arms clinging desperately to his shoulders, his tongue thrust aggressively, catching her off guard. She groaned as she felt his legs wrap around hers, holding her so close she was startlingly aware of his every muscular reaction.

She hung on to him frantically, off-balance and over her head. Her thin cotton shirt was no barrier at all, and she was vitally conscious of the feel of his flat, hard stomach against hers, conscious of the thrust of her breasts against the hairy texture of his chest.

Benjamin laughed softly against the corner of her mouth, galvanizing her into action, but when she would have slithered from his grasp, one of his hands came around to cup her buttocks and press her tightly against him. The feel of his arousal was incredibly exciting, and she gasped, swallowing a mouthful of water as she attempted to tear herself free. His hands grew still.

"Better now?" he murmured.

"Benjamin, d—"

His mouth closed over hers once more, shutting

off her protest, and she fought a silent battle against the sweet coercive power of his lips, his tongue. The dark, currentless waters conspired to hold them in physical contact, even when one of his hands left her back to slide up under the front of her shirt.

His fingers brushed over the tightly furled bud of her hardened nipple and spread to encompass her breast, and she could feel the instant response of his body. Panicking, she hammered on his shoulders, thrashing desperately in his grip.

"Damn it—" He broke off, holding her helpless against him as he stroked with one arm toward the shore. When he stopped again, it was plain that his feet were firmly on the bottom, but Chalis still out of her depth. She could only cling to him. Her hands slipped on the satin smoothness of his wet skin, and her fingertips dug into his resilient muscles. Her legs drifted up, and he reached down with one hand to urge them around his body. His hand slid up to cup her buttock and lingered to slide under the loose leg of the trunks, and at his intimate touch, she began to push against him, whimpering an incoherent protest.

"Chalis, Chalis, stop it, sweetheart!" he murmured huskily. "You'll sink us both."

She twisted her head aside, kicking out in an effort to disentangle herself. "No, no—*please*, Benjamin!" she gasped.

"You're really frightened," he murmured wonderingly. Slowly, he allowed her to slide out of his grip.

Away from his touch, sanity began to temper her unreasoning panic. "I should have known better!" She paddled awkwardly until she could touch bottom and then surged ashore, slipping and sliding on the soft, silty bottom. "It's a pure reflex with you. You forget—I've seen you in action!"

In the darkness, her lashes spangled by water, she tripped on the wrought-iron foot of a bench and swore loudly. Coming silently up behind her, Benjamin swatted her behind. "Watch your tongue, girl."

She flung around to confront him. "I don't play games, Benjamin. If that's all you have on your mind, then maybe you'd better stay away until after I've gone back to New York!"

The furious silence assaulted her ears, inviting the doubts to rush in on her before she could shore up her defenses. So he had made a pass at her; it meant less than nothing to either one of them, but it was best to set the record straight at the beginning. Under no circumstances was she going to get involved in Benjamin's favorite water sport! She was here to sort out her whole future, both personal and professional, and a one-night stand with a man who, in his own words, liked to keep things casual, wasn't going to do much for her powers of concentration.

Gleaming wetly, Benjamin towered over her. Chalis could almost feel the waves of hostility radiating from his body. There was nothing at all gentle in his touch when he caught her to him, slamming her against the cold, hard surface of his body. "Don't make the mistake of confusing me with other men, Chalis," he ground out. "If that's all you think of me, if that's the impression you've carried around all these years, then maybe I'd better live up to my reputation!"

Throwing out reckless words in a desperate act of

self-defense, she jeered, "All these years? Don't be so damned egotistical! I'd forgotten you even existed!" Which was a blatant lie, but she was in no condition to be reasonable.

Starlight glinted on the silver in his wet hair, on the drops of water on his sleek shoulders. As if mesmerized, she stared at the dark shadow of his face until the stars were blotted from the sky. His mouth came down on hers, thrusting apart her lips to assault the vulnerable softness with an aggressive tongue. In silent, tense anger, they dueled on the most primitive level, his masculinity intent on asserting its dominance over her.

Finally, she could take no more. Sagging against him in surrender, she felt his muscles slacken, and the assault was slowly withdrawn. If there was an element of hesitancy in his withdrawal, in the way his lips seemed to linger momentarily on hers before lifting, the way his hands seemed reluctant to relinquish her body, she put it down to imagination. She was too shaken to be angry, too drained to be anything more than relieved.

He left her with a terse oath and an equally terse word of apology, but she hardly heard either of them. Gravel spurted as he reversed his truck and turned around, and then he was gone.

She lay awake for ages, and when she finally slept, she slept heavily. When she awoke, her thoughts flew immediately to Benjamin, and she pushed him determinedly from her mind. Today had better be filled with activity. There was a time for introspection and a time to avoid it, and she knew instinctively that this was one of the latter.

The drive to Winston-Salem took little more than thirty minutes, and it carried her through some of the loveliest countryside in the Piedmont. Unconsciously, she slowed down as she passed the entrance to the Poe farm, Yadkin Trace. It overlooked the river, and she had never seen more than what was visible from the highway. It had never occurred to her to wonder just how extensive it was. Enormous cedars burdened with rambling Cherokee roses and honeysuckle had all but obscured the fences. Evidently Benjamin was too busy to bother with landscaping—or too poor. Farming was an uncertain business at best, as well remembered from her own childhood. A chicken truck from Wilkesboro was riding her bumper, and she put her foot down and moved on.

The day proved unexpectedly enjoyable. She wandered through the beautifully landscaped Reynolda Gardens, looking into the shops that had opened there, and visited two of the city's several excellent galleries. The caliber of work in both surprised her. Somehow, living and working in New York, she had forgotten.

A quick trip to the bank was enough to remind her that she couldn't afford to indulge herself forever. Sooner or later she'd have to face up to either going back to New York and marrying Walt, or resigning her job. Her shoulders sagged. The thought of beginning at the bottom again was unbearable, but if she didn't marry Walt, then she could hardly go on working for him. There must be some rule of etiquette to cover such situations.

There were still a few days before she had to decide. She'd forget it for now and go on drifting until she felt she could trust her decision-making apparatus again. Benjamin wasn't the only one who had learned to doubt his judgment in such matters. It was a lot easier to avoid entanglements in the first place than to go through the painful process of extrication after the fact.

Approaching the clearing again, she heard the sizzle, caught the drift of hickory-flavored smoke even before she saw the gleam of the silver pickup through the trees.

"Hi! I tossed these on as soon as I heard the sound of the gate. Hope you've brought your appetite home with you." His eyes sought hers searchingly, the silent message in them speaking more clearly than words.

"Benjamin!" Surprisingly enough, there was no anger left, just a feeling that was amazingly like relief. Besides, it took only the delectable aroma of broiling steak to remind her that she had forgotten to eat lunch. How the devil could she treat him with the disdain he deserved when she was starving?

"It occurred to me that with the barometer falling, the fish might not be biting this afternoon. From the looks of you, missing a single meal might be fatal." The teasing note served to place them back on comfortable ground once more, and Chalis relaxed. Not even the slow, appreciative survey he conducted could get under her skin today.

"I hope there's something to go along with the steak." She hid any remaining wariness under her social smile.

"How about sweet onions, homemade grape leaf pickles and Hungarian red wine?"

Tossing her purse onto the table beside the two pewter steak plates and the appropriate cutlery, she sighed. "Heavenly! I forgot lunch."

"Several lunches, from the looks of you," he observed dryly, turning the huge slabs of beef over on the grill he had brought outdoors.

"I intend to make up for it," she warned him. "What can I do?"

The steak was prime Angus, hung almost three weeks, he told her later as she unashamedly gnawed the bone, and the onions were as mild as any apple. The wine was a little more robust than she usually preferred, but it seemed perfect tonight. "Where'd you get the pickles?" she asked, munching on her third one.

"My housekeeper supplies them by the gallon. She's the world's worst cook, so I guess she has a secret supply. I don't ask questions."

"Bootleg pickles. Hmmm, sounds enticing."

His grin was contagious. "You and your craving for forbidden delights!"

They had chosen to eat outdoors. The evening chorus had started up again, and the sky to the west of them was lit by almost constant flashes of lightning, silhouetting the graceful skeletons of several dead elms that towered over the dense growth across the pond. There was no trace of the tension that had splintered between them last night. Under Benjamin's easygoing friendliness, it had completely dissipated.

"I'd better heat some water to wash your dishes," she murmured, stirring herself reluctantly.

"Don't bother." Benjamin stood and gathered the

things together, placing them inside the straw hamper he had brought. He poured the last of the wine into the two crystal glasses and handed her hers.

"Hmmm, this reminds me of when Gran Ada used to picnic with us. She could never abide paper things. We always used china and crystal and even linen napkins."

"I remember her. Miss Ada had a lot of style." He smiled, and Chalis fought against the potent combination of his comfortable friendliness and his powerful virility. "So do you," he added quietly.

A simple "Thanks" would have been appropriate, but for some reason, Chalis was unable to utter it. The tension was back, the poise that had always come to her rescue lamentably absent. She jumped nervously to her feet and muttered something about getting a sweater.

"We'll go inside for coffee if you'd rather. The mosquitoes are coming out, anyway. Here, you might want to rinse your hands off in the bucket before I douse the coals." He handed her a paper towel, and she tried to think of some excuse not to prolong the evening. Eating steaks outside with him was one thing; she wasn't sure she was up to sharing coffee with him in the intimate confines of a candlelit cabin.

He was one step behind her, reaching for the matches before she could come up with something clever about eating and running. "How about using the lantern, and we'll save the candle for emergencies," he murmured, tilting the slightly smoked chimney.

"Cozy," he remarked, looking over the dimly lit

room. The jade green linen she had worn on the plane hung from a hanger on a nail, and she had pushed her suitcase, with all her other clothes inside, under a bunk. "I've never actually spent a night here in all the years I've been coming here to fish and swim."

"That's a bit hard to believe," Chalis said witheringly, perched on her chair, and he laughed softly.

"Ahh, my reputation as a playboy." Oddly enough, even after the way they had parted last night, there was no sting in the remark. "That's one I'll have a hard time living down, isn't it?"

She shrugged, watching the play of heat lightning outside. "Why bother? With no wife to worry about, what difference does it make?"

"It might lift the eyebrows of a few friends," he ventured.

"I can't imagine why."

"Can't you?" His voice was a gentle rasp, a hint of indulgence mingling with the speculative note. "Can you deny that it bothers you?"

"But then, I'm hardly one of your friends."

Benjamin stood and moved over to the hearth to put the kettle on the gas burner, pausing to arrange the coffee things on the table nearby. "Would it bother you if I smoked an extremely mild cigar in here? I find the occasional one helps calm my nerves."

There was a momentary flicker of the tension that seemed to ebb and flow whenever he was around, and than it drained away again. "Help yourself. Not that I think for one minute that your nerves need calming," she added derisively.

The small flare of a match highlighted his strongly carved features, momentarily casting intriguing shadows across his face. He blew a thin stream of fragrant smoke toward the window and settled himself more comfortably against the bank of pillows she had heaped on the spare bed. "Maybe I'm just nervous when I'm around someone who tells me she doesn't consider herself a friend."

Startled, Chalis tilted her head in a characteristic gesture to stare at him. "Who, me?"

"You," he replied evenly.

"Oh, but I didn't mean it that way. I mean, we're not *not* friends, if you know what I mean. It's just that you were so much older—well, not actually all that much, but you know what I mean. You were always far too busy with other interests to pay any attention to a—"

He picked up the sentence and finished it for her. "To a big-eyed, big-eared, long-legged kid, who was entirely too eager to learn the facts of life," he finished softly, an odd, almost indulgent note in his voice.

"If I stared, darn you, it was because you and your giggling harem kept frightening the fish away!" She couldn't subdue a small giggle of her own. He was absolutely right. She had been far more interested in Benjamin's conquests than in any piscatorial pastimes. "I must have been an awful pest. It's a wonder you ever got any courting done."

He shrugged. "It's Kenyon property. We have a small pond at Yadkin Trace, but the fishing—not to mention the courting—was always better here." He stood to pour the coffee, handing her a mug and resettling himself. "Tell me, Chalis, what's been going on in your life that's honed you down to bare bones and raw nerves? I can't honestly say city life seems to agree with you."

If there was an edge in the drawled observation, it didn't prevent Chalis from a shockingly unexpected desire to unload her problems on Benjamin's accommodating shoulders. Before she could voice the automatic rebuff, however, he continued.

"You're touchy as all get-out. It doesn't take a degree in psychology to figure out that something's wrong. If your job's secure, then it must be personal; and if a disinterested party can be of any help as a sounding board, then feel free. I promise you, I'm not easily shocked."

"Oh, I don't think so," she protested hastily, breathlessly. "But thanks." Her smile—that invaluable mask she had cultivated so assiduously—was brilliant, belying the sudden turbulence inside her. The light from the lantern deepened the shadows under her cheekbones, darkening her large, luminous eyes to obsidian.

Benjamin stared at her for a moment longer, almost as if seeing her for the first time, and then he shrugged and stood. "You're the doctor. I'll check in from time to time to be sure you're all right. If you need anything, you know where I live."

4

By noon the following day, Chalis was far too restless to settle for a lazy afternoon spent fishing or simply drifting around the pond on a float. This time she'd head for Mocksville, perhaps stop in and visit with Aunt Steffie, and pick up a few items from the grocer's.

Recognizing, if not quite understanding, an obscure need to make contact with Walt, she pulled in at the drugstore. Selecting a picture postcard from the rack and purchasing the necessary postage, she continued through town to the prim white house where her aunt and uncle lived. The front door was closed, but, just to be sure, she walked around the spacious yard to see if the car was in the back.

It was gone. There was obviously no one home, and Chalis admitted to herself that she was glad. She hadn't really wanted to talk—it was just the need to touch base with her relatives. For reasons she preferred not to explore, she had awakened that morning with a set of brand-new insecurities.

Sinking onto the slatted wooden swing, she set it into motion and removed the postcard from her purse. She really should have called before now. Walt had been extremely forbearing throughout all her emotional ups and downs. Jorge would have dismissed them as scathingly as he had dismissed any other show of emotion. After eighteen months of marriage, he had left her with feelings of inadequacy that would take years to overcome, in spite of her successful career, in spite of Walt's flattering attentions.

Smithson and Leigh, the lawyers who handled Jorge's estate, were one of her worries, along with Walt's proposal. She had panicked when she had been summoned to their offices and presented with the news that Jorge had died and left her everything. Either he had known how much she'd hate it and had done it deliberately—Jorge had a distinct talent for subtle cruelty—or he had simply forgotten to change his will again after the divorce. Either way, it had come as a stunning blow to her. In the end, she had simply walked out and refused to discuss it. There were other odds and ends of the estate, but they could all be dealt with by the lawyers as soon as she felt able to instruct them; she knew now what she was going to do. Meanwhile, she'd put the whole thing out of her mind.

Setting the swing in motion with a restless shove, she nibbled the top of her fountain pen. She was sorry now she had given in to the impulse to get in touch with Walt. Thinking of any one aspect of her situation brought down the whole mess on top of her head, and she was just plain exhausted.

"Drat!" she muttered irritably. What could she say to him on a postcard? "Having a wonderful time, wish you were here," she enunciated slowly, scrawling the message across one side of the card. What else could she say? She wasn't ready to accept or reject his proposal yet.

Scribbling a note to Aunt Steffie, she clipped it to the hanging note pad on the front porch and walked out to the mailbox with her card. A sigh lifted her shoulders as she raised the flag. The simple action took her back to a time when life had seemed so safe, so uncomplicated.

Oddly enough, from this distance it was Walt who seemed safe and uncomplicated. She had enormous respect for his intellect as well as his business acumen. Moreover, Walt had his emotions under perfect control. While he might not exhibit much warmth, neither did he indulge in the scathing diatribes that Jorge had directed at her with increasing frequency before she had worked up her nerve to walk out on him.

Walt had not attempted to press her at first. It was only when she'd started falling apart at odd moments that he had shifted their relationship to a more personal level.

While he was an attractive man, Walt was not as handsome as Jorge had been. His features were nice but unremarkable, his eyes a clear, rather pale shade of blue, and his soft black hair was going slightly thin on top. But he was tall and gentle and soft-spoken, and she had learned the hard way to mistrust handsome men with devastating charm.

Walt had proposed to her on the afternoon when she had come from seeing Smithson for the first time. She had been stunned all during the taxi ride back to the gallery. By the time Walt joined her she was seated at her cluttered desk, staring at her burnt orange filing cabinet with tears streaming down her face. He had held her, comforted her and elicited the whole story from her. When she had kept repeating over and over that she didn't want the damned collection, didn't want *anything* of Jorge's, he had asked her to marry him and let him handle all her worries.

Now, remembering that day a few weeks earlier, Chalis grimaced. There was some consolation in the fact that she had been able to focus her thoughts on the situation for more than two consecutive minutes. Lately, her mind had recoiled whenever she tried to think about what to do about Walt and about Jorge's legacy.

"Nothing's ever simple anymore," she muttered, passing the grocer's without even seeing it. If she turned down Walt's offer of marriage, she'd probably have to give up her coveted job. And why did she keep thinking in terms of turning him down? She was extremely fond of him. They got on marvelously!

But did she *want* to be married? Did she *need* another man in her life at this point? She was certainly well able to support herself, and as for the other—the sex—that whole aspect of marriage was vastly overrated.

When Benjamin drove up early in the afternoon,

Chalis was floating around the pond on the yellow raft, counting the small, puffy clouds as they drifted overhead and disappeared beyond the surrounding treetops. She resented being jarred out of her reverie.

Benjamin waved a casual salute and waded through thigh-high grasses to the upper arm of the pond. She lost sight of him, but from time to time she could hear the plop of a lure striking the water. Stubbornly, she remained where she was. He had a key. He could go and come as he pleased, but she didn't have to be hospitable.

Her fingers made agitated little movements through the water, and after a while it occurred to her that she may as well go ashore. Any hopes of further relaxation were shot, at least for now.

The pickup truck drove off just as she clambered up the slippery bank, and she stood there and stared after it blankly. Then she burst into tears—the first time she had cried in days.

Benjamin came again just before dark the following evening. Chalis was fishing. She had boiled half a dozen eggs the night before, but after breakfasting and lunching on them, she was ready for a change of diet.

"Catching anything?" he greeted her, wading through the tall grass to where she stood casting her unwanted lure out again and again. He wore a pair of work-stained khakis that conformed to his leanly muscled body with rather stunning faithfulness, and his arms, several shades darker, gleamed with a fine sheen of perspiration.

"They're not biting," she announced flatly, dragging her gaze away from him to eye his tackle box and spinning rod with grim satisfaction. If they weren't biting, they simply weren't, and all Benjamin's easy expertise would be as futile as her own more amateur attempts.

"Then we'll have to make them an offer they can't refuse, won't we?" He opened the tackle box, a veritable treasure trove of colorful lures, and surveyed the contents.

"This I've got to see. Prominent plowboy attempts to bribe local largemouth," she muttered derisively.

He grinned down at her, his lazy hazel eyes glinting with tolerant amusement. "Don't knock it, honey. To catch what you want to catch, you have to be smarter than your quarry. That's where you and I differ."

"At least you don't have to worry about drowning," she said witheringly. "If you ever fall overboard, your inflated ego will keep you afloat for hours."

Smiling in bland acceptance of her jibe, he unclipped the swivel from the end of the monofilament, tied a fresh loop in it, and then selected a plastic salamander, which looked exactly like the real thing. "Feel," he murmured, handing it to her before working it onto the weedless hook.

It felt fleshy—soft, resilient and amazingly alive. She dropped it as if it had burned her, and he studied her briefly with an exasperatingly knowing smile before stepping several feet away and making his cast.

"You have to think like a fish," he told her,

lowering his voice to a confidential murmur. "I always choose my bait carefully, place it close enough to where my victim lies waiting, and then I bide my time."

Chalis watched in growing impatience as he stood there, allowing the salamander to sink beneath the mirrorlike surface. Still he didn't begin reeling it in. "Aren't you going to do anything?" she demanded finally.

He shook his head, that oddly disturbing smile still lingering on his lips. "I never rush things. Can't risk scaring my victim off before it's time to sink the hook." He lifted the tip of the rod and took up the slack. "Just an occasional twitch, a little something to tantalize and intrigue. If the bait's picked up, we go from there."

They waited together, and Benjamin's eyes never left the line that floated across the surface of the water to where his lure had sunk to the bottom. Chalis realized she was holding her breath. She also realized her attention was not on the fishing line, but on the man before her.

Moving restlessly, she stood up just as Benjamin motioned for her to be still. "He's taken the bait," he whispered, and she watched in growing amazement as he fed out line with swift, efficient motions. "We let him run with it. He's picked it up by the tip of the tail, not at all sure he wants it. But his curiosity is aroused; that's the first step."

"But the hook's in the other end!"

"Exactly. Now if I can keep him from suspecting a trap, he'll take it to where he feels safest, and then he'll think about it for a while before he begins to turn it around in his mouth. A bass swallows his meal head first."

There was a sudden flurry of motion, and then Benjamin was reeling furiously. The tip of the rod bent double, and the sound of the rachet sang out loudly as he moved swiftly to gain a better position at the edge of the water. Chalis watched in stunned admiration some minutes later as he netted the chunky largemouth bass that must have weighed all of seven pounds.

"I don't believe it," she breathed. "I could have sworn they weren't biting, and on your first cast . . ."

"Native wit." He grinned, releasing the fish by lowering the net beneath the surface. "We simple country boys are known for it. I guess by now you've had all your rural edges polished off, but maybe I can teach you enough to keep you from starving while you're here."

Chalis gazed at the spot where the bass had disappeared with an arrogant flip of his broad tail. Then she turned to stare at the man who was calmly putting away his tackle. "Hey, I could have done with a fish dinner!"

"Would you settle for country ham sandwiches and mangos for dessert?"

Her stomach moved a notch nearer her backbone and she glared at him. "Why didn't you say you had food? Here I wasted all this time watching you show off."

They devoured the sandwiches, three for Benjamin and two for Chalis, and Benjamin kept both wineglasses filled.

"I'll be up drinking water all night after this ham," Chalis murmured, finishing off her third glass of wine.

"There's a lot to be said for simple pleasures," he murmured, a soft gleam in his narrowed hazel eyes. They had dined inside tonight by unspoken mutual consent. "But then, I guess you're pretty bored with it all by now, ready to head back up north to all the excitement New York has to offer."

It was a leading statement, and Chalis's guard was down. She allowed herself to be led. If she needed to talk things out—and she did—then who better than Benjamin? He was someone from her warm and comfortable past; totally unrelated to any element of her present situation, he'd be completely objective. Lord knows, there was no one else she could talk to. Except for Tansey Williams, Walt's secretary, she had lost touch with the few friends she had made in the early days, and Tansey was half in love with Walt herself, even if she wasn't aware of it.

It was easy to speak into the shadowy, lantern-lit quietness. Outside, there was no traffic noise, no strident screams of sirens—only the nightly chorus of crickets with the occasional rhythmic bass of a bullfrog. The very absence of pressure acted as a vacuum, drawing the words from her in an increasing stream until she had voiced all the more overt problems that beset her.

"The estate is easily handled," Benjamin said after a period of silent consideration, a period in which Chalis was dimly aware of a weight being lifted from her shoulders. "After probate, the collection can be given away and the investments used to pay the residual taxes and the administration. It shouldn't require much more from you than your signature."

"Walt offered to handle it for me," she murmured, allowing her eyes to close momentarily.

Candlelight gleamed on the healthy sheen of Benjamin's chest through the careless opening of his khaki shirt. "Walt," he said. "I suppose that's the next item on the agenda. Do you love him?"

Chalis's eyes flew open, and she craned her neck to the other bunk. "How do I know if I love him?" she demanded irritably. "I thought I loved Jorge! What do I know about love?"

"Hmmm . . . I know the feeling," he mused. "So what about the sex? Do you enjoy sleeping with him?"

Cupping the lower part of her face in her hand, Chalis turned to stare bleakly out the window beside her bunk. "We don't," she said flatly. Beyond her mirrored image, she could see Benjamin's head swivel slowly around to stare at her.

"Not at all?"

Wordlessly, she shook her head.

"Why not? Or does he have other preferences? And if he has, then what the hell do you hope to gain by marrying him? It can't be money. Not if you're giving away your inheritance."

"Oh, for goodness sake, it's nothing like that," she muttered. "It's just that we don't—I don't—well, it's simply not that important!"

"Sex is not that important?" he marveled slowly. "Honey, how old did you say you were?"

"You know damned well how old I am, and it's

beside the point! You earthy types always put everything on a barnyard level!"

"Speaking purely as a cow farmer, I'd say it was a pretty practical level. At least none of my prize breeding stock has developed a tendency to burst into tears lately."

"Well, I'm not one of your fancy heifers," she snapped, "so suppose we end this session right now!"

Ignoring her outburst, he stood up and stretched, throwing his powerfully built torso into magnetizing relief. "Mmmm, good idea. I'm in the mood for dessert. How about you? A big, juicy mango? Freshly picked just yesterday."

It was an easy escape from an awkward situation; it would have been churlish to refuse. Besides, mangos were one of her weaknesses. "I've never been able to get enough," she admitted, swinging her long legs off the bunk. "Unless you've invented a nonmessy way to eat them, I'd rather tackle mine outdoors."

"Trust me. There's only one way to eat these things." His hand went to his belt and he paused, cocking an eyebrow at her. "Do you swim in that rig?"

Puzzled, Chalis looked down at the faded orange, pink, purple and green trunks. "I told you I don't own a bathing suit. I sort of appropriated these from the nail behind the door—my all-purpose back-to-nature costume."

"Avery's," Benjamin informed her laconically. "His taste hasn't changed much, unfortunately." He unzipped his khakis and stepped out of them before

Chalis could avert her eyes, and she saw with relief that he wore the same brief trunks he had worn before. He tossed his shirt onto the bunk along with his pants and dropped a casual arm over her shoulders as he led her outdoors.

Chalis moved jerkily away from him, vaguely conscious of a disquieting flutter in her stomach. "I take it we eat first, then douse each other with buckets of water? Unless you've been hiding the fingerbowls from me?" She opened the top of the hamper he had brought with him, reaching in to stroke the plump oval fruit.

"Oh, honey, trust me to know a better way than that. I learned the proper way to eat mangos al fresco a long time ago, and believe me, it's not a style Miss Ada would have approved of. But if you're game . . . ?" He selected two of the largest mangos and unsheathed a knife. "Come on. Didn't I see a couple of air mattresses down by the edge of the water?"

"The green one leaks." She felt the instinctive need to fling one last toy arrow, reluctant to admit how much she was enjoying Benjamin's company.

"Then I'll be chivalrous and let you have the other one. I have my ego to keep me afloat, after all."

She grinned unrepentantly, picking her barefooted way down to the edge of the pond. There was a half moon rising over the upper end, casting a pinkish glow on a skein of wispy clouds. The idea of eating the tropical fruit afloat was too enticing to resist; and, after all, they'd be on separate air mattresses.

"Wade out and board your vessel, madam. I'll peel this creature for you, and then you're on your own."

He stood knee-deep and peeled his own before shoving his float out into the water. Neither of them spoke for several minutes as they drifted together and then apart again.

Chalis finished first. Sitting upright, her legs dangling, one on either side, she held up her sticky, glistening hands and groaned, "Oh, this is pure heaven! You know, Ben, for a cow farmer, you do come up with some fantastic ideas."

He swung about and paddled over beside her, reaching out to capture one of her wrists. "What's the matter, did I leave a few hay seeds in my hair? I thought you'd forgiven me my rustic beginnings," he taunted. "Hmmm, you're a messy eater, aren't you?"

"And you're the soul of fastidiousness, I suppose. Oh—" She caught her breath in a shuddering protest as he carried one of her hands to his mouth and began to lick the sweet juices from her fingers. "Ben, stop it!"

"Waste not, want not," he murmured, allowing his tongue to follow the honeyed trail to the palm of her hand.

The sensations that ran rampant through her body were unbelievable, and she jerked her hand away, tucking it behind her as she stared at him with eyes gone suddenly wide.

He laughed softly. The moon was behind him, but she could see his strong teeth gleaming palely as his gaze played over her face. "You always did have hungry eyes, even as a child. Round, brown and shiny, like big chestnuts."

Paddling to a safe distance away, she managed to get her voice under control. "I never knew you even saw my eyes when I was a child."

"Oh, I saw 'em, all right—peeping through the bushes, usually. Half the time when Avery and I came down here with a couple of girls, all you Kenyons were in residence, and we'd have to wait until after you'd gone to come back for our—uh . . ." He deliberately left it dangling, and Chalis, feeling more secure dealing with the distant past than the disturbing present, countered easily.

"Your *uh?*" she teased. "I hope we didn't make you wait too long, but then, you'd have been perfectly welcome to join our picnic. Gran Ada thought you and Avery were the sweetest boys."

"Oh, we were, I assure you! I have any number of testimonials."

Astride her air mattress, she leaned back, her legs still dangling over the sides. The water was like warm black silk caressing her lightly tanned skin. A bat darted close to the water and swerved upward again, and at the other end of the pond, a fish's jaw snapped noisily on some hapless insect.

"Chalis?" Benjamin said tentatively.

She didn't want to be disturbed. Bliss wasn't all that easy to come by.

"Chalis, my air mattress is sinking."

"You'll float," she told him succinctly. "Your ego, remember?"

"You punctured it with your pointed remarks about my lowly station," he informed her in a suspiciously plaintive tone—and from considerably closer. "I guess we'll have to double up. I couldn't go the distance to shore so soon after eating."

Before she could react, he had transferred his weight aboard her shaky raft, almost swamping them both in the process. She clutched at his shoulders as she struggled to maintain her balance, kicking out as they threatened to turn bottoms up.

Quivering to a more or less stable position, the ends of the mattress curled up to cup their backs. They were seated facing each other with arms entangled for mutual support and balance. "Don't move," Benjamin warned her.

"Don't even speak to me!" Chalis snapped, seething with amusement and indignation and something else that didn't bear analysis. She twisted her head backward in an effort to put a bit of space between them.

"Whoa! Be still!" he whispered. "I think the heron's back." He removed his hands from her shoulders, only to slide them under her thighs and lift them so that they rested on his own. The small action brought them closer together than ever. She was practically sitting astride his lap.

Confused, she peered over his shoulder to where a large white blur had settled in one of the alders that rimmed the dam. Benjamin reached around her to paddle the raft to a better position for viewing, and each stroke meant a contact that seared her vulnerable flesh.

"Benjamin," she whispered frantically.

"Hush," he murmured, lifting a hand to cover her mouth. His fingers strayed until one of them broke the barrier of her lips and slipped inside her mouth. Her tongue moved to eject it and remained to caress it until, with a groan, he gathered her even closer to him and, covering her mouth with his, replaced the finger with his tongue.

There was a dreamlike quality to the whole sequence. Neither of them dared move quickly for fear of capsizing, and Chalis surrendered the last grain of her common sense on that flimsy pretext. She kissed him hungrily, savoring the taste of his flesh, the bold aggressiveness of his tongue. It was as if she had been starving and were intent on devouring every morsel.

Her hands bit into his back, and when he removed them, leaning slightly away from her in order to slip her sodden shirt over her head, she whimpered a protest. Instead of gathering her to him again, he leaned back, his hands clasping her narrow rib cage, and gazed at her, and her own eyes fell before the hooded intensity of his. Her breasts, small, high and firm, gleamed like pale, inverted flowers in the moonlight, their crests resembling a darkly furled calyx.

"Benjamin," she pleaded, her voice cracking uncertainly.

"Relax, honeylove—you're among friends."

"I—I don't feel very relaxed."

Wryly, he admitted, "Neither do I, at the moment." His hands moved up to touch her lightly, the fingers stroking across the nubs of her breasts until she could have screamed from the silvery tension that gathered in the pit of her stomach. And then, before she realized what was happening, he leaned sideways, carrying her with him into the silent dark depths of the pond.

5

It was unlike anything she had ever experienced before. Benjamin swam with her, a lazy sidestroke that engaged only his powerful legs and one arm. With the other arm, he held her close to him—so close she could feel every muscle in his flat abdomen and his powerful thighs as he propelled them shoreward. Their legs tangled and slithered apart and tangled again.

"Benjamin, you're insane," she whispered hoarsely, barely managing to keep her mouth clear of the water. Her arms were wrapped about his waist.

"Hush, my sweet, long-legged water witch. You'll drown us both."

She gave up, turning her head so that her face was uppermost, her cheek pressed against his throat. She could have drowned in the scent of his healthy male flesh, the warmth that simmered beneath the cool surface of his skin.

He carried her ashore; she could never have found the strength to climb the sloping, silty bank to the rough softness of the dew-wet grass. "My shirt," she wailed helplessly.

"I'll bring you one of Avery's," he promised, amusement shimmering huskily just under the surface of his voice.

Tonight the air was warmer than the water had been, but she was chilled. She *must* be chilled. Why else would she be trembling uncontrollably?

"Come inside and let me dry you off," Benjamin growled softly, leading her inside the warm, dark cabin.

Her towels hung on nails behind the door. He reached for them, not relinquishing his grip on her arm, and draped one across her head, the other across her naked shoulders.

"I'll light a candle, shall I?"

The match flared, and Chalis turned away. She couldn't look at him, not after the way she had responded to his lovemaking. "It must be a conditioned reflex, where you're concerned," she reiterated, rubbing her hair with unaccustomed ruthlessness.

He removed her hands from the towel and began drying the ends of her shoulder-length ash blond hair. "What are you grumbling about?" His voice was gently teasing, his hands as efficient as if he dried a woman's hair every day of the week.

"Take one Benjamin Poe; add one female, any type; mix with water, and presto—instant sex!"

The hands on her scalp stilled momentarily before resuming their task. They were seated on one of the bunks, and Benjamin had braced the top of her head against his chest for easier access. "Hmmm—I'd forgotten my lurid past."

"Well, I hadn't. Just because I'm now of age and happen to be on the spot doesn't mean I'm available." She felt compelled to throw up a barricade of words.

He raised her head and looped the towel around her neck, smiling with infuriating complacency. "All right, Chalis, you call the shots." Instead of Chalis, to rhyme with Alice, he pronounced her name as Shallie, and it sounded oddly like an endearment. "Some women expect that sort of thing, you know. Far be it from me to disappoint a lady."

"Well, I'm not some women," she asserted, her defensive hackles lowering reluctantly. She almost wished he had tried to force the issue. Then she would have been justified in running him off the property. "I told you before, sex doesn't particularly interest me. I have more important things on my mind. While I appreciate your taking time to drop by now and then, I'd just as soon not get sidetracked by any rustic Romeo who thinks he owes it to every woman he takes swimming to try and seduce her."

The light wasn't particularly good, and what appeared to be a flash of amusement in Benjamin's hazel eyes was probably no more than a blaze of irritation. At any rate, Chalis wasn't about to apologize. She searched her mind for a polite way of ending the evening. She needed time to come to terms with the irrational way she was reacting to his advances.

"Has Leonard been by recently?" Benjamin asked, throwing her off-balance by his calm acceptance of her put-down. "Steffie doesn't like for him to come fishing alone—not since his heart attack." Benjamin leaned back and reached for his pants, removing his cigar case from the pocket. "Mind if I smoke?"

Stunned, she ignored the question and he lit up, uninvited. "Heart attack," she echoed weakly. "What heart attack?"

"Oh, it wasn't a big one—angina, I think—but you know Steffie. Now that the kids have all left the nest, Leonard's her one chick and child."

"Why wasn't I told?" Chalis was distraught. Her uncle had been like a father to her since her own father's death.

"I don't suppose they thought it was necessary. The kids all checked in from time to time, and your cousin Charles was here for a month or so. He looked after things for Steffie."

She couldn't let it go. Doubling her legs under her, she sat there, totally unselfconscious in the garish drawstring trunks, a towel and nothing else, and stared morosely at the glowing tip of Benjamin's cigar. "I was so wrapped up in my own concerns, I guess I let time get away from me."

"I know, girl. Don't blame yourself. With a career to consider, and your love life to sort out, it's no wonder you can't keep track of the day-to-day happenings down here in Davie County."

Benjamin left soon after that, and Chalis walked him out to his truck. He gave her the other mango and told her he'd bring more in a day or so, but she hardly heard him. Her mind was on her favorite uncle and the fact that no one had even thought to contact her at the time. Was she so selfish and uncaring? Had they thought she'd be too caught up in her own affairs to be interested in her own family? *Were* her priorities actually that fouled up, after all?

Leonard Kenyon drove up just before noon the following day. "Thought I'd see how you were faring," he greeted her. "Had a phone call from a friend of yours last night."

She had left his phone number in case she had to be reached, but she hadn't expected to hear from anyone. "Who was it?"

"Gentleman by the name of Gregory. Sounded like his shoes were about two sizes too small for him."

She laughed, strolling with her arm around the thickening waist of the stocky, balding man. They sat down on a weathered bench in the shade of a black walnut tree. "Now that you mention it, he sort of does," she gurgled, swallowing a small surge of guilt. "Do I need to call him back?"

"That's up to you. He gave me a message to pass on. Here goes: 'Quit stallin' and come on back here where you belong. Corticelli needs you and so do I.' That's it, near as I recall." He stretched an arm along the back of the bench. "Who's this Corticelli? For that matter, who's the fellow with the tight shoes?"

Extending her legs out in front of her, Chalis

allowed her head to fall back against her uncle's arm as the laughter bubbled forth. If the laughter threatened to edge over into tearfulness, it was only for an instant. She restrained the impulse easily—definitely an improvement over her lack of control these past few months. She was getting stronger.

"Corticelli is the name of the gallery. The man with the tight shoes is Walt—Walter Harriman Gregory—my boss." She'd elaborate on the relationship when and if the occasion arose. For the moment, she was more concerned with other matters. "Uncle Leo, why didn't you tell me about your heart?"

Leonard left some forty-five minutes later, promising to come fish with her if he could get away from his wife's eagle eye. "Wants to baby-sit me," he grumbled. "Managing woman!"

Feeling reassured as to her uncle's health, Chalis dug into her suitcase and came up with a tiny pan of watercolors, a Chinese brush and a block of paper. She painted several extremely bad watercolors, thoroughly enjoying herself, until the leading edge of a thunderstorm drove her back inside. She was rummaging around in the ice chest for something to eat when Benjamin drove up. Parking the truck as close as possible to the cabin, he dashed inside, flinging raindrops in all directions.

"You're worse than a Saint Bernard," Chalis declared, handing him a towel. It was getting slightly gray. She'd have to make a trip to a launderette tomorrow. "Did you bring me anything to eat?"

"Greedy creature! I offer you my handsome face

to admire and my sparkling wit for your edification, and all you can think of is your stomach!" He loped back out to the truck and returned with the straw hamper and two bottles of wine.

Chalis took the bottles from him and leaned over the table to peer into the picnic hamper. "At least I have my values properly sorted out," she parried with a teasing glance. There was a round of soft cheese, two more mangos and something wrapped in foil that smelled almost like . . .

"Ribs! Barbecued spareribs! Benjamin, you absolutely adorable man!"

"This promises to be a messy feast, with your lack of facilities. Unless you like to swim in the rain, that is."

"I'll set the water bucket under the downspout," she murmured, removing the ribs, the cheese and several mysterious containers from the basket. "Why don't you do it for me, since you're already wet?"

He complied, returning a moment later muttering something about being used, and Chalis, with a spontaneity she hadn't felt for years, brushed a quick kiss against the square thrust of his chin.

"There, there, you know you love it. Doesn't everyone want to feel needed?"

They pulled the table between the two bunks and opened all the containers. Chalis placed a stack of paper napkins nearby while Benjamin uncorked one of the bottles, and they sat cross-legged on the two bunks, eating, laughing and talking. "There's just no civilized way to eat these things," she complained when Benjamin reached across to wipe a smear of sauce from her chin.

"Depends on your definition of civilized. The bone-gnawing tradition has a long, noble history."

They progressed from there to a discussion of politics, theosophy and a controversial novelist whom Chalis had met at a recent cocktail party. It wasn't until considerably later that it occurred to her that Benjamin was a surprisingly stimulating conversationalist—for a cow farmer.

Somehow, Chalis found herself laughing more than she had in years. Without her having been aware of it, laughter seemed to have faded from her repertoire just lately, but Benjamin's finely honed sense of humor meshed with hers so neatly that time and time again he reduced her to helplessness.

"I haven't laughed so much in years!" she declared.

"Don't you laugh with your friend, Walt?" he asked, uncorking the second bottle of wine.

"Oh, Lord, no! Walt's a serious person. We appreciate the same sort of things, mostly, but I don't think I've ever seen him really cut loose and laugh."

"What about your husband?"

"Jorge? Oh, Jorge thought any show of emotion—*any* emotion—was gauche. The only time I recall his being amused was when he had put something clever over on another collector. . . ."

She broke off, her mouth drooping unconsciously, her fists clenched in her lap. Benjamin reached over and gently unfolded her fingers. "Let your hackles down, honey. You're bristling from nape to tail."

"Jorge," Chalis announced lugubriously, "*never* used terms like 'tail.' Anatomy embarrassed him, I think."

Benjamin observed quizzically that there seemed to be quite a few things Jorge never did—a statement that Chalis, even in her considerably mellowed mood, could hardly deny.

Slightly unnerved by his steady, contemplative scrutiny, she rushed into speech. "Uncle Leonard came by. He said Walt had called."

"Have you reached a decision yet?" Benjamin stood up and closed the window over his bunk. The rain was beginning to blow in. He moved around the cabin, testing each one, and then settled down at the foot of Chalis's bunk. "Are you going to marry him?" he asked quietly.

Fidgeting with her glass, she looked away. "I still have a week to decide," she evaded.

"Have you stacked the pros against the cons? He doesn't laugh with you; he doesn't make love to you. Have you figured out just how the pair of you are going to spend all your time together?"

Twisting over to stare out at the boisterous thunderstorm, she tried vainly to lose herself in the monotonous drumming of rain on the roof. "Oh, how do I know? We have dozens of things in common!" she exclaimed.

His hand was a gentle weight on her ankle, not stroking, merely curving around the delicate bones with an insidious warmth. "I'm your friend, Chalis. I hate to see you make another big mistake. We both know from personal experience that a bad marriage can take a pretty heavy toll."

She flung herself around, her eyes imploring in the yellow lantern light. "How can I *tell,* Ben? Give me one good, foolproof test."

His hand smoothed up the length of her shin to cup her knee. "If it were all that cut and dried, there'd be no such thing as divorce. But from the perspective of hindsight, I'd say that before you consider casting your lot in with another person, you should be pretty well acquainted with yourself. How well do you know yourself, Chalis?" he persisted.

"I've better things to do than dwell on my own shortcomings!" Swinging her feet to the floor, she mumbled something about coffee, and Benjamin caught her wrist, tumbling her onto his lap.

"Don't evade the issue, Chalis. We both know perfectly well why you're running." His deep, slightly raspy drawl registered on her spine with telling results, and then, before she could evade him, he turned her head and found her mouth.

In a single instant, she was changed from a creature of reason into a mass of compelling needs. The only reality was Benjamin's arms holding her, his mouth moving sensitively over the contours of her lips. He didn't immediately seek to deepen the kiss. His hands were warm on her back and her shoulders, and her breasts felt correspondingly cold as she craved his touch there. His mouth brushed gently back and forth over hers, and a low sound escaped her lips. She could feel the swiftly accelerating beat of his heart slamming its contagious rhythm into her own pulses.

For agonizing moments his kiss remained a tenuous, teasing thing, as if he were memorizing her mouth with his lips, intent on knowing every curve and indentation.

A tremor coursed through his hands as the muscles of his body tightened against her in response, but it was Chalis, when she could no longer bear the shimmering, crystalline tension, who broke the bonds of his restraint. Her mouth opened under his and he groaned and bore her down onto the hard mattress, pinning her willing body with his while his hands began the task of unbuttoning her blouse.

It was as if once the restraint was broken, he couldn't get enough of the taste of her, the feel of her. He sucked at her bottom lip and then moved on, his tongue caressing the line of her jaw and the soft, vulnerable flesh under her chin. "Chalis, Chalis, you're so damned delicious!" he groaned against the frantic pulse at the base of her throat. His hands had laid open her blouse and were now claiming her breasts, stroking the pink silk of her nipples into hard points of desire.

Swiftly, with unsteady hands, he removed her shorts, and she lifted her hands to push his shirt upward. Laughing shakily, he completed the action, tugging it hurriedly over his head and tossing it aside.

In the shadowy darkness, his trousers followed the shirt, and Chalis's gaze moved hungrily over his beautiful, gleaming flanks. Her legs shifted instinctively, allowing him to settle himself intimately against her. He kissed her deeply, almost desperately, and then his mouth moved slowly down to her breast, leaving behind a glittering trail of sensation as his lips closed over the demanding peak. With slow, tantalizing swirls of his tongue, he assuaged the aching need in her breast, only to rouse other, more demanding needs in other parts of her body.

"Ben, oh, please—oh, yes," she sighed, unaware that she had spoken aloud. He was fondling the delicate angle of her hipbones, and then his hand swayed down into the hollow of her abdomen as his mouth closed over her navel. She trembled uncontrollably, her breath coming in raw gasps as the point of his hot tongue found a center of unbelievably exquisite sensations.

Her hands closed over his shoulders, her fingers digging into the hard, resilient muscles. As he loomed above her in the near darkness, she slipped her hands downward, combing through the pelt of crisp body hair on his chest to find the tiny constricted points. He shuddered, swearing under his breath, and then he came down on her with his full weight, and she gloried in it, craving to know every inch of his magnificent body. Hard shudders racked his tense frame as she shifted awkwardly in her attempt to accommodate herself to the overwhelming new demands her body was making. She was only dimly aware of his hesitation. "Tell me what you want me to do, Chalis," he rasped.

Bewildered, she stared up at his hooded face, her mind unable to cope with mere words. This was not a time for words, for demands and decisions. It was a time to quench this insane inferno that raged out of control inside her. "Benjamin, please . . ."

"Tell me. Do you want me, Chalis? Do you want me to make love to you? Do you want what I can give you—want it with your mind as well as your body?"

Half in shock at the tumult of conflicting emotions that coursed through her, she continued to stare at him. What sort of game was he playing, for God's sake? "Don't you want me?"

Abruptly, he sat up and, turning his back on her, leaned over to rest his head on his fist. She could see the glisten of sweat on the muscles of his back, could actually see the slight movement caused by the hammering of his heart. Distraught, she lifted a hand and touched his side, and he jerked away, rising to his feet to stalk across to the door. The sound of his breathing was clearly audible. The rain seemed to have stopped, leaving behind a stillness fraught with explosive tension.

"Benjamin?" she murmured tentatively.

"Forget it, Chalis. In case you were worried, though, take my word for the fact that you're a normal woman—in every way. I'd advise you to think twice before tying yourself to any sexless wonder, no matter how much he has to offer in other departments." His words scraped her nerves like a serrated blade, leaving her raw and hurting, totally unable to cope with this new and devastating sort of pain.

Too shattered for anything except complete honesty, she spoke again. "Benjamin, what is it? Did I do something wrong? I—I guess I'm not all that experienced, but—"

"Chalis—" He broke off, his voice harsh with an emotion she couldn't begin to define. Exasperation? Disappointment? "Chalis, my God, it's like taking a virgin! It's been a long time since I've wanted a woman as much as I want you, but I don't think I can handle the responsibility—for either of us."

At her continued silence, he turned to her, a look

of anguish on his face. "Chalis, it's too soon. You're not ready for this, regardless of what you think right now, and I've just discovered that I'm not, either. Let's just take things a little slower, sweetheart."

He laughed abruptly, and the sound was like tearing cloth. "Remind me of those words the next time I do my damndest to get you into bed, will you?"

With that, he left. Gathering every vestige of pride at her disposal, Chalis stood in the door and watched his shadowy form stride across the clearing. "Stay away from me, Benjamin," she yelled after him. "Just don't come back until after I've gone!"

She couldn't be sure the words had reached him, couldn't be sure she even wanted them to, but he paused for an instant before slamming himself into his truck.

6

The lack of stiffness or soreness in her muscles almost came as a surprise the following morning, for emotionally, Chalis felt as if she'd been run over by a steamroller.

Assaying a rueful smile, she raked her fingers through her tangled hair. Rain had always made her sleepy, and it had rained off and on all night, but it had been hours after Benjamin drove away before she had been able to doze off.

The plain truth was that last night had been a staggering revelation to her. She had never reacted to any man the way she had to Benjamin. Maybe it had been the wine, or a combination of everything. Whatever it was, it had gone to her head in a way that had taken her completely by surprise.

Poking about in the straw hamper Benjamin had left behind, she munched on leftover grapes and cheese biscuits as she tried to evaluate her reactions in the sober light of day. Anger? No, not really. Whatever had happened, it was pointless to pretend that she hadn't been a willing partner all the way—a little too willing. It had been Benjamin who called a halt, not she. She wasn't used to being left cliff-hanging that way, but then, she'd never climbed so high before. And as exhilarating as it had been, the experience would not bear repeating.

She'd just have to brash her way through their next meeting and thank her lucky stars that Benjamin had had the good sense to back out when things had threatened to get out of hand. As embarrassing as it was, she'd be darned if she was going to turn tail and run just because she had had a little too much wine and made a fool of herself with someone she had known all her life.

Wandering out to the edge of the pond to watch the morning mist being burned off by the clear hot sun, she wondered about Benjamin's marriage. What had gone wrong? She had a dim recollection of an extremely pretty little brunette: pink and white complexion, voluptuous curves in a minimal bikini, and a breathless way of squealing every few minutes. How on earth had a man of Benjamin's obvious intelligence and discernment gotten tangled up with a cotton candy doll?

Chalis returned to the cabin, and, dressing in her one remaining clean outfit, she gathered up everything that needed laundering and plopped it in the backseat of her little rental car. It was easy enough to rationalize spending another day away from Quarter Moon Pond. There was the laundry to be done, for one thing, and galleries she hadn't even seen.

It was almost dark when she got back to Quarter Moon, and she was disconcerted to discover the gate had been left unlocked. Normally she was extremely careful about locking up, both going and coming.

The pulse at the base of her throat was fluttering even before she caught sight of the familiar gleam of silver through the pines. All day she had held at bay the thought of what had happened the night before, of how she'd feel when she had to face Benjamin and pretend that she hadn't been devastated when he had drawn away at the last possible moment.

The sound of laughter reached her as she opened her door, and she stood there, unwilling to acknowledge the disappointment that surged through her at the realization that he wasn't alone. That was going to make this first meeting even harder to face.

Or would it? Perhaps she should consider it a reprieve.

"Chalis?"

It was her aunt's voice. "Coming, Aunt Steffie. Let me get my packages!"

She strolled into the clearing, her social smile already in place, and then it wavered and fell as Walt came to meet her. She dropped the pillowcase of laundry from numb fingers. "Walt . . . What are you doing here?"

"I think it might be more in order for me to ask where on earth you've been all day. Do you realize that I've been here for hours?"

One hand lifted to brush over her eyes, as if to wipe away a hallucination. A parody of a smile flickered across her lips and faded, and then she moved forward, her shock quickly controlled as she reached up to kiss Walt's cheek lightly. "How lovely to see you," she murmured, turning to greet her aunt and uncle even as her eyes moved beyond them, seeking another face.

Benjamin allowed the lure to sink beneath the surface, his mind on the low murmur of voices that came through the woods at his back. God, of all the breaks—to have Gregory turn up *now!* He had known who it was at first glance, even before Leonard had introduced them.

Something bumped his lure and Benjamin reeled it in carelessly, then laid the rod on the grass beside him as he sat and stared out over the lower end of the pond. What were those two doing now? Was she still greeting him? With kisses, no doubt, although how she could even consider marrying a cold fish like Gregory was beyond him! If he had proved anything to her last night, it was that she was too much woman to settle for less than a man.

He pulled out a cheroot and lit it, frowning at the stream of blue smoke that drifted out to disperse on the still air. If he were smart, he'd cut through the woods and get the hell out of here right now. He'd done his good deed, for old times' sake. Damned near lost his head in the process, too!

Who would have thought he'd end up making a pass at one of the Kenyon kids. The tall, skinny one, at that! She'd never been actually pretty when she was a child, but there had been something about her, a sort of wide-eyed gravity that he had found oddly appealing. Nor had he had much trouble recognizing her after all these years. He hadn't remembered her name, but he had remembered watching her stalk around the pond like a long-legged shore bird. There had been a certain delicacy, an awkward young gracefulness. And her eyes . . .

Uttering a short, rude word, he flung the cheroot into the water. He could kill the bastard who had put those shadows under her eyes! Once, a long time ago, they'd been full of healthy curiosity—full of laughter and the sort of confidence that came from knowing yourself loved and accepted. Now, it was as if she had sealed herself under glass, only peering out on rare occasions. She was beautiful. Oh, God, yes; she was beautiful enough now for any man. But it looked as if she had completely lost confidence in herself as a woman, and that was a damned shame.

Raking his fingers through his hair, Benjamin stood up, an expression of determination on his face. For old times' sake, for all the good times he had had here at Quarter Moon as a boy, thanks to her grandfather, he owed her one.

Shouldering his spinning rod, he strode through the woods to the clearing, his eyes swiftly taking in the scene around the table before they caught sight of him.

Chalis sat on a folding stool, her long legs drawn up before her, staring out over the water with a withdrawn expression on her face that Benjamin found disturbing—almost painful. Ten minutes, and the bastard had done this to her, put that distant look on her face, as if she were a beautiful mechanical doll.

"Benjamin! Come on over here, boy, and have a seat." Leonard gestured to the bench.

"Thanks, but I expect I'd better be running along. The fish aren't hungry, but I'm beginning to get that way myself."

Chalis turned slowly to look at him, her eyes devoid of expression, and his gaze narrowed on her with a determined glint. He'd be damned if he'd let her get away with ignoring him, with pretending that last night hadn't affected her as much as it had him! It was something more than masculine ego that prompted him to invite them all to dinner.

Chalis sat across the table from Walt and tried to follow the thread of conversation. Her mind had reverted to a pattern that had become all too familiar, as if she were reaching for something that continued to elude her.

Leonard and Steffie had begged off, claiming a civic club meeting, and it had been obvious that Walt had not been particularly thrilled at the idea. Nevertheless, without being openly rude, there was no way they could get out of Benjamin's unexpected invitation, since they obviously had to eat somewhere. He had apologized for not having them at Yadkin Trace, explaining that his housekeeper was at her worst in the kitchen.

Unashamedly allowing her attention to stray from a discussion of the latest political flap, Chalis stared unseeingly out across the room of the small, exclusive restaurant.

"What do you think, darling?" Walt broke into her absent meanderings with the coolly intimate tone he adopted when they were with others. At her blank look, he went on to say that Benjamin had invited them both to be his guests at Yadkin Trace until they returned to New York.

"But, Walt, I'm already settled," Chalis protested, conscious of Benjamin's look of polite disinterest.

"Don't be absurd, Chalis. If I'd had any idea of the appalling conditions of that—that wretched shanty, I'd never have allowed you to leave New York."

She bit back the retort that rose to her lips. Nothing would be gained by arguing about it. Walt was one of those irritating individuals who simply ignored opposition.

"You'll be comfortable there, even if I can't offer you much in the way of meals," Benjamin assured them blandly.

"Oh, but I—"

"Well, thank you, but we—"

Chalis and Walt spoke at the same time, and Chalis broke off with a helpless feeling that she was no longer in complete control of her immediate future. It was not a feeling she enjoyed. "Look," she managed before Walt could continue, "I think I'll just stay put; but, Walt, why don't you take Benjamin up on his offer? We can have our meals out. I can even cook you a fish dinner one night."

"God forbid," he intoned feelingly.

The waiter arrived with their dinners, and the discussion continued on a desultory level as they dealt with superbly prepared *mignonettes* of beef and braised wild mushrooms. The men had coffee and Chalis decided on half an orange poached in syrup and served with cream, candied ginger and chocolate curls. She rearranged the garnish with her spoon while Walt held forth on the investment possibilities in art and antiques.

"We can all go back to Quarter Moon to collect your things, Chalis," Benjamin offered after signing the check. Ben had left his truck at the pond and was driving Chalis's rented car, instead.

"Thanks, but I'm sticking. Walt"—she turned to the urban Northerner with an almost imperious lift of her chin—"I'll come by for you at about ten in the morning and we'll take it from there, all right?"

It was obvious from the heightened color in Walt's normally pale cheeks that it was anything but all right.

On the drive back to Davie County Chalis closed her eyes on the view of two sets of shoulders, two masculine heads, each so damned arrogant in its singular way. It was not so easy to close her mind, however. Walt was here, and she didn't want him here; she wasn't ready yet. Seeing him out of context, as it were, was disconcerting enough, without having Benjamin's quiet presence confusing the issue. The contrast between the two men was both subtle and obvious, and the differences were not at all those she would have expected.

They stopped at the gate, and Chalis automatically got out to unlock it. For a moment after Benjamin parked the car beside his own truck, the three of them sat silently. The moon, slightly more than half full now, shone down over the treetops, lending an unearthly beauty to the pond and the lacy branches of the dead elms beyond.

"It shouldn't take you long to get your things

together. I believe, if you don't mind, I'll wait here for you. Lord knows what's lurking out there in all that jungle," Walt announced.

Which was not precisely a chivalrous stand to take, she thought with wry amusement. "Don't worry about me. We have a resident king snake," she told him, swinging her long legs out the narrow opening. "He takes care of the copperheads."

"My dear Chalis, I do hope you're joking." Walt shuddered fastidiously.

Benjamin slid out and came around to join her. "I'll help you close up shop, Chalis." He pronounced it Shallie again, and she had a sneaking suspicion he did it deliberately.

"Walt, you and Benjamin go on. I meant it when I said I didn't want to pull up stakes. I'm all settled in here and I love it. It's what I came home for. We'll hit the high spots tomorrow. There are a few galleries in the area that might surprise you."

Walt's indrawn breath was clearly audible. "Chalis, please—it's been a long day and I'm not in the mood to indulge you while you play camp fire girl. Whatever Poe's farm is like, it can't be as bad as this overgrown mudhole!"

Chalis, hands bracing her slender hips, glared down at him through the window of the car. This was a Walt she had never met before. Oh, she had seen him angry often enough, but she had never known him to be openly rude. For the first time, he reminded her of Jorge, and she found it rather frightening.

Benjamin was standing by silently, his lean, sinewy form relaxing against the door of his truck. It occurred to Chalis that if he could have located a straw in the darkness, he'd have been chewing on it, with a slightly wicked glint of amusement in his eye.

"We'll collect the rest of your things tomorrow," Walt went on petulantly. "Now, if you don't mind, I'd like to try and get a few hours of sleep! We have seats on the twelve-forty. I changed your reservations before I left the airport."

Benjamin parked the pickup truck under the old-fashioned porte cochere beside the house. There hadn't been more than three words exchanged on the drive back to the Trace, but Gregory's thoughts had been perfectly evident. He hadn't liked Chalis's final refusal to follow orders, much less her stubborn refusal even to discuss the matter. Benjamin had the small satisfaction of knowing that she had not appreciated Gregory's high-handed attitude.

So far, so good. Now, unless the bloodless bastard somehow managed to convince her to leave with him tomorrow, he'd guess that she was well on the way to coming to her senses. It might not be particularly fair to judge a fish out of water, but here was one fish he was going to do his damndest to show up for what he was—fair or not.

7

After scrubbing herself dry, Chalis dressed in her batik skirt and the black halter. She brushed her hair until it crackled around her head before deftly tucking it up in her habitual French twist, and then, makeup kit in hand, she headed for the one and only mirror on the property, the one in her car. A dab of lipstick on a naked, suntanned face had served well enough before, but now she needed the armor of a complete paint job in order to face up to Walt and tell him she had no intention of cutting her vacation short by so much as five minutes. Nor was she ready to accept his proposal.

The tire was flat! And she had deliberately taken her time in bathing, not coming out until her fingers were shriveled and pale. Now, half an hour late already, she had waltzed out to the car, makeup case in hand, only to find the thing sagging there in an off-balance lurch, a vaguely apologetic look on its chrome-faced grill.

Well—there was nothing to do but change the thing. Here's hoping she still remembered how. Wrinkling her nose at the little compact car, she decided it would be a cinch, only she realized she'd better step out of her skirt and halter first. She was already beginning to wilt under the double-barrel charge of heat and humidity. Glancing around quickly at the silent, empty woods, she stripped down to her single undergarment, a pair of black bikini pants, immediately feeling the coolness engendered by the breeze on her damp skin.

In the small, sunny *cul de sac* in the midst of the grove of pines and persimmons, she positioned the jack and began to pump. The sun felt good on her naked back. In fact, nudity felt surprisingly good. Already she could feel the knots of tension at the back of her neck beginning to ease. It was going to be another scorcher—it already was. At this rate, she thought, panting as she struggled with the jammed hubcap, she'd have to take another swim before getting dressed again.

She had removed two lugs and was cursing the idiot who had machine-tightened the third one when she realized she was not alone. Rocking back on her heels, she wiped a trickle of perspiration from her eye and looked up into Benjamin's bemused face. "What in the devil do you mean by sneaking up on me like this?" she blazed out.

His thick, silky black brows lifted in surprise. "Coming from *you* . . ."

"Oh, skip it! You might at least have the grace to

turn your back until I get some clothes on!" Standing swiftly, she swayed as the combination of heat and hunger struck her.

He steadied her with a hand on her shoulder, and she jerked herself away from him. "Look, Chalis, you'd better cool off—in more ways than one." He reached through the window of the car to where she had left her clean clothes. "Get dressed if it will make you feel more comfortable, but head for the shade."

"I can't put those on now," she wailed, wiping a greasy hand across her dripping face. "Look at me!"

"I am." A slow smile kindled in his hazel eyes as they ranged slowly over her lean frame, taking in the small white breasts that were only partially covered by her crossed arms. Her hips flared sweetly from a narrow waist, and the cut of her black nylon underwear emphasized the length of her golden tan legs. "Tell you what—" He paused to strip the navy knit shirt over his head. "Put this on for the sake of your modesty and go wait for me in the shade by the pond. I'll change your tire for you, and then we'll both get cleaned up and go find something to eat. I've been up all night with a sick friend, and as tempting as your naiad outfit would be any other time, you're perfectly safe. Changing a tire, with maybe a bit of simple voyeurism thrown in, is about all I can manage on an empty stomach."

"A sick friend?"

"Forget it. She's fine now, but you're going to be flaking out in a minute if we don't get you out of this sun. Now, scat!"

Feeling suddenly too drained to argue, Chalis took

the shirt, shot him a withering look and turned away. She could feel his eyes following her as she picked her way through the wild blackberry vines and blue-eyed grass, but she refused to stop and put on the shirt while he watched. A sick friend, indeed! He must have a terrific bedside manner!

By the time Benjamin joined her, she was sitting in the lush grass at the very edge of the pond in the shade of a huge, lightning-scarred oak. She had pulled the shirt on over her head, acutely conscious of the scent of his body, the slight dampness of perspiration that clung to the soft fabric.

"All done," Benjamin announced quietly, dropping down beside her. Her peripheral vision took in the magnificent spread of his shoulders. Sweat had trickled down the center of his chest, emphasizing the **V** pattern in the thatch of dark curls, and Chalis forcibly prevented her gaze from following it down to the intricate brass buckle of his wide leather belt.

"Thanks. I appreciate it. Not that I couldn't have managed it alone."

"Of course," he said gravely.

"Of course," she echoed, her lips quirking into a grin in spite of herself. "Seriously, Ben, what are you doing here? Have you been working at Dutchman's Creek again?"

"No. Matter of fact, I'm here because your friend Walter was worried about you. You're running late, you know. It's almost eleven-thirty."

"Oh, Lord, his plane," she groaned.

"Don't worry about that. I managed to convince him not to race back to New York just yet. You can thank me later for rescuing the rest of your vacation. He was all set to shanghai you aboard the same flight."

"Thanks, but it wasn't necessary. I'm not that easily pushed around, you know." Her tone was dry, and she turned quickly away from Benjamin's look of amused skepticism. "Look, it's true! Whether or not you believe me, I'd have flatly refused to go back until I was good and ready."

And Walt would have turned huffy; one thing would have led to another, and she'd have been out of a job before she knew it. My God, she thought in awed amazement. And I was actually considering marrying the man?

Suddenly, in the clear morning sunlight, she had a subliminal glimpse of the future she had marked out for herself. A kaleidoscopic swirl of impressions rushed over her. One thing stood out plainly, however—she didn't have to marry any man just because she couldn't think of a logical argument against his constant subtle pressure.

"Did you know that the sun causes red and blue highlights on your hair that make it look almost lavender? You've grown into an extremely lovely woman, Chalis," Benjamin observed as impersonally as if he were calling her attention to a dragonfly on a button bush.

Her spurious poise deserted her, and she moved restlessly, hugging her knees to her chest. "I'm not really pretty, you know. Well-groomed, maybe; smart, if you're generous; but—"

"Hmmm, well-groomed. Precisely the term I was reaching for," he informed her judiciously. She felt his eyes move to her muddy bare toes, to the sweat-stained shirt she wore over her underpants, and on to the streak of grease she had unknowingly transferred to her forehead. The twin devils that ignited in his eyes were too much for her, and she retaliated, leaning forward to scoop up a handful of the rich wet muck that edged the pond. Before he could duck away, she plastered it onto his chest.

When she inadvertently touched a hard, masculine nipple, his eyes narrowed to a blaze of fire that had her scampering to escape. "That'll teach you to make fun of me!" she jeered a little shrilly as she launched herself into the water to escape his reaching arms.

He was right behind her, pausing only long enough to shuck his khakis. The briefs he wore were definitely not bathing trunks, and she dragged her eyes from his powerful masculine body and struck out for deep water. He caught up with her easily, in spite of her efficient crawl.

"Oh, no you don't—not after I came to your rescue and changed that tire for you."

Suddenly, it was as if all the intervening years had faded out, leaving a younger Benjamin and a magically transformed Chalis in a situation she had wasted hours daydreaming about as a girl. Her fingers slipped ineffectually off his sleek wet shoulders, and he hauled her against him, laughing down at her from moisture-beaded eyes. "If we're dealing in mud baths—"

"We're not, we're not!" she cried, twisting against him in an effort to escape his hard grip.

"Then if all you want is to swap massages, I'll be

glad to oblige." He leered playfully. His hand was already moving up under her shirt—*his* shirt—and he was laughing as hard as she was. Strangely enough, the whole incident was almost totally asexual. His hands on her body felt good—they felt wonderful—as did his legs entwining with hers, his hard, flat torso sliding past hers as they wrestled to remain afloat. They were like two healthy young animals at play.

"I sweat and slave and work my fingers to the bone . . ." he admonished, laying a hard, well-shaped hand against her face and pushing her under.

She came up sputtering to grab a handful of his hair. "Not to mention giving me the shirt off your back, and other well-known clichés."

He wrapped his arms around her shoulders, trapping her arms. "And what's the thanks I get?" he growled down at her, so close she could see the fine lines raying out at the corners of his eyes. "A fistful of mud!"

She giggled, ducking under his arms to come up grinning at him from a safe distance away. "My sincere and heartfelt thanks, Benjamin," she intoned with mock piety. "But I *could* have changed it by myself, you know."

"Yeah, well . . . it's just a good thing *I* came after you instead of your city slicker boyfriend." He rolled over to float on his back, legs crossed at the ankle, and Chalis trod water and gazed at him, admiring the sleek gleam of his hard muscles.

"Why didn't he come after me instead of you?" she asked, trying to picture Walt changing a tire—or drifting around a farm pond in his shorts.

"Afraid he'd get lost. I left him in the front parlor looking at pictures, but if we don't get a move on, I'm afraid he'll call out the cavalry." He grinned irreverently and headed shoreward in an easy crawl that ate up the distance with no appreciable show of effort.

Chalis followed, her weather-vane spirits unaccountably sagging deeper with every stroke. "Hurry," she muttered, as Benjamin stopped to scoop up his pants.

He led the way to the cabin and tossed her one of her own towels, using the other on himself. Chalis allowed the small presumption to stoke her temper, as if instinctively recognizing the need for anger as a barrier between them. The atmosphere was suddenly entirely too volatile to be safe; it could ignite from a single look, and she was a firm believer in safety first.

Ignoring her hastily contrived hostility, Benjamin stepped into his pants and zipped them up, drawing in his hard, flat stomach as he fastened his brass buckle. He frowned as he lifted the sodden shirt Chalis had peeled off.

Turning her back to him, she fumbled in her suitcase for a dry pair of pants. "Look, would you mind getting out of here while I get dressed?" she snarled.

"Something's obviously bugging you. If the idea of getting dressed is going to rile you up that much, why don't you just stay as you are? I'll risk it if you think your boyfriend's blood pressure can stand it."

"Leave Walt out of this!"

"I'd be delighted to!" he muttered angrily under his breath. "Unfortunately, one of us is going to have to deal with him in short order!"

He strode out, slamming the door behind him, and Chalis's defenses caved in like paper dragons. Dear God, what ailed her! One minute she was as happy as a clam, and the next she was snarling like a rabid dog.

Chalis turned in between the rocky flanks of the farm entrance. Today she was blind to the lush beauty of the rampant flowering vines and the ancient cedars. Her mind churned relentlessly as she followed Benjamin's truck. She shouldn't let him get to her that way. But was it Benjamin? Or Walt? Or herself? It was an unfortunate combination of all three, she thought wryly, slowing automatically for a cattle guard.

The driveway into Yadkin Trace was much longer than she had imagined. She was grateful for the distraction as she wound through broad, hilly pastures, neatly fenced and dotted with sleek black Angus. Partly hidden beyond a stand of tall willow oaks she could see the roofs of several well-kept outbuildings, including an enormous hip-roofed barn.

Yadkin Trace was turning out to be considerably larger than she had thought, and so far they hadn't even reached the house. Benjamin had told her simply to follow his lead. At this rate, they'd be in the next county!

The house appeared suddenly. Its rambling design followed a natural ridge overlooking the river as if it had grown there over a period of years—which was little less than the truth, as she later discovered. Slowing instinctively, she admired the unassuming loveliness of Benjamin's home. Odd that she had never associated him with this sort of background, and yet, it fit.

The house was not new, nor was it of any particular style. It was long, white and two-storied, with lots of French windows and porches; there were balconies on both levels, some screened, some glazed and some open. Rooms jutted out at odd angles, as if the house had grown a bit with each season's sun and rain. And yet, it all blended in with a charming wholeness, held together by an assortment of vines that reached out toward an overgrown boxwood garden.

Pulling up under the clematis-covered porte cochere behind Benjamin's truck, Chalis let herself out before he could come around to open her door. "Come along, I'll take you to your boyfriend and then see what I can round up for lunch. Pearl's bound to have something ready by now, I'm afraid."

"I wish you'd stop referring to Walt as my boyfriend," she snapped, following him into a small square room.

"Sorry." He strode on through the room, calling out to his housekeeper that they were ready for lunch.

Following him hesitantly across the cool stone floor, Chalis's eye was caught by a tall, narrow print half hidden behind the jungle of houseplants. She shoved back a stalk of geranium and peered closer. It was an original serigraph, and a very effective one, too. Not her favorite medium—she preferred something more direct—but extremely well conceived, all the same.

Inhaling the spicy scent of geranium leaves on her hand, she looked around for other prints and was not disappointed. Before she had time for more than a cursory glance, however, Benjamin was back with Walt.

"There you are, dear. Come see what I've discovered. Poe tells me he knows some of these artists personally. There's one—but come see for yourself."

She recognized the symptoms. Walt was almost animated. It took something like this, the possibility of a new artistic discovery, to bring a flush of excitement to his pale features.

Benjamin excused himself to go change into something clean and dry, and she felt Walt's soft palm on her elbow. "Come along, darling. These serigraphs are predictably banal, but wait until you see the pastel. Poe *can't* know what he has here, and before I leave this bucolic little paradise, I'm going to have one L. Maurice signed up for a one-man show. What's our schedule like after the first of the year? Could we possibly shuffle Rankin and Todd to a later date to make room for—"

"Walt, you know as well as I do that we're booked solid for the next three years!"

"We could make it a three-man show instead of a duo," he grumbled, but Chalis shook her head.

"The publicity's already in the works."

"All right, but just tell me this . . ." He gestured to a large, lushly colored pastel of several skillfully drawn nudes posed kaleidoscopically against a patterned background of ferns and Oriental rugs. "Am I supposed to ignore an artist of this caliber when I could sell everything he turns out before it's even hung?"

So this was what Ben had meant when he said he'd left Walt in the parlor looking at pictures. That droll wretch! Swallowing a tendency to giggle, Chalis studied the work for long, silent minutes. Then she moved to consider other works in the same room, and then she took in the room itself. It was large, comfortably shabby, with well-worn linen slipcovers over what appeared to be very good furniture. The walls were a warm white, the dark wooden floors covered with an eclectic assortment of colorful rugs, and there were at least a dozen paintings of varying quality on the walls. Periodicals, books and a large Steuben vase of full-blown peonies added the final touch, and Chalis was aware of a sudden powerful affinity for the room—for the whole house. She could have curled up on that long sofa and napped contentedly.

Benjamin rejoined them before she could venture an opinion of the work. "If you're ready to brave lunch, it's on the table," he told them resignedly.

"This L. Maurice person," Walt murmured politely as he followed Benjamin into a small sunny breakfast room. "There's a certain degree of promise there—a bit raw, but he shows an engaging—ah—naïveté. I'm not sure, but I just might be able to give the fellow a boost. Encouragement at this stage is vitally important to a budding artist."

Chalis bit her tongue and avoided looking at either of the men. She knew Walt's approach by heart. Downplay the interest, proceed slowly from indifference to patronizing indulgence, and then, when the prize was within reach, move in for the kill, armed with contracts that would sew up every mark the artist made on paper or canvas for the next hundred years. Walt always insisted on exclusivity in his artists.

Benjamin's smile intruded on her feigned interest in the casserole, and she looked up to meet it. "Sorry about this," he murmured, nodding toward the baked offering, which seemed to be a study in grays: greenish gray, pinkish gray, and something vaguely taupe. "Dessert, Pearl tells me, is canned peaches—the high point of the meal, except, of course, for the possibility of botulism."

"You mentioned being personally acquainted with several of the artists you've collected?" Walt persisted, helping himself to a generous serving of Pearl's ambiguous offering. "Would you—ah—happen to know anything about this Maurice fellow?"

Benjamin buttered a saltine and handed it to Chalis, then buttered another for himself. "That would be Lara. Yes, as a matter of fact, she happens to be a rather good friend of mine. Why?" he asked with an innocence that caused Chalis's eyes to drop in swift amusement.

He knew precisely what was going on, she realized. But then, any man who had managed to put together such a strong collection as she had found here would be no easy mark.

Benjamin handed her another cracker and she smiled her thanks. He nodded toward the bowl of coleslaw—long-dead cabbage embalmed in mayonnaise. She shook her head. She'd wait for the peaches. Walt was going on about the bare possibility of persuading one of the lesser galleries in New York to take a look at the pastel and possibly even make an offer for it—as if he'd allow any other knowledgeable dealer within a mile of one of his discoveries!

"Of course, Corticelli has certain standards to maintain, you understand," Walt murmured apologetically. "I couldn't promise to involve myself personally—at least, not officially."

At the same moment, both Chalis and Benjamin noticed that Walt had devoured large servings of the casserole and the wilted slaw while he pursued his quarry with single-minded intensity. Chalis struggled to keep her lips from quivering and hastily averted her face to avoid Ben's eyes. It was as if they were communicating—even laughing—in a silent language against the background drone of Walt's monologue.

By the time the peaches were served—home canned, topped with thick, unwhipped cream, and unexpectedly delicious—Benjamin had tactfully refused Walt's offer for the nudes, but he had agreed to call his very good friend, Lara Maurice.

His *very good friend.* The words echoed silently inside Chalis's head as she watched him leave the room, moving with that lithe, masculine gracefulness that was so characteristic of the man. She became aware of a small, painful twinge that had nothing at all to do with incipient food poisoning.

After arranging for them all to join his artist friend

for an impromptu dinner at her studio later on, Benjamin offered to conduct them on a tour of his farm.

"No, no. Chalis and I have certain important matters to discuss," Walt declared firmly. "I'm an extremely busy man, you know, and as delightful as it might be to visit the—ah—barnyard under other circumstances, I'm afraid I must decline for us both. No offense, my dear fellow."

8

Like the other parts of Benjamin's house that Chalis had seen, the library was imbued with his personality. Underlying the ambience of generations of Poes was a richly masculine atmosphere of leather and cheroots. One of Benjamin's books was turned face down on the leather sofa, and there was a tray containing a decanter and two used champagne glasses that Pearl had not yet removed. Chalis wondered who had shared a drink with him—and when. Nearby, a tall silver and cut-glass pitcher held a single magnolia blossom, an incongruous feminine touch in a bachelor household.

Chalis thought of the little she recalled of the woman who had become Jean Poe. How long had Benjamin's marriage lasted? What had happened to end it? Had they lived here? She found herself hoping intensely that they had not, and then she rebuked herself for being oversensitive.

She continued to stare at a series of framed photographs of Angus bulls while her unruly mind wrestled with an awkward tendency to linger on Benjamin Poe. She needed to be gathering her self-confidence for the interview ahead. It would have been better if she and Walt could have met to talk somewhere else—at the airport, for instance, or an impersonal restaurant. Anywhere but here, with Benjamin's littered desk before her, his Western style straw hat tossed casually onto one of the worn leather chairs.

While Walt selected a seat, pinched the creases of his sharkskin slacks and settled himself with a slightly irritating deliberateness, Chalis braced herself to decline his offer of marriage with as much grace as she could muster.

"Chalis, I understand from Poe that you aren't planning to go back with me tomorrow. Could I possibly persuade you to change your mind?"

She edged gingerly onto the chair facing him, wishing she had taken time to apply her makeup after her second swim of the morning. She needed all the help she could get. "Walt—"

"If not," he went on heedlessly, "then I'd like to suggest that you empower me to act for you on the Smithson affair. You see, there's a small but extremely desirable collection of miniatures coming on the market next week that would fill out Jorge's—"

"Walt!" Dismayed, Chalis could only wonder at his utter lack of sensitivity.

He held up a staying hand, its palm pink and as smooth as Chalis's own. "Now, darling, I know you don't want to be bothered with all that detail. I only want to save you the worry, and as probate ends shortly, I thought we might use a few of the municipals as collateral and—"

"Walt, stop it! I've already decided how to handle Jorge's estate. I appreciate your concern, but you see, I—I couldn't in all good conscience accept it when I'm sure Jorge didn't really intend for me to have it. I've been thinking. At his age, a will wouldn't have seemed so important. He probably didn't even remember until too late that he had changed it after we were married, so you see, under the circumstances . . ."

"No, I don't see! Jorge would be the first to want his collection in the hands of someone who could appreciate it. The Modiglianis alone would be worth a small fortune!"

"Walt! Listen to me. I'm going to give the collections to Jorge's *alma mater,* and the investment portfolio can be used to pay administration costs. For all I know, the university will have to build special facilities. These days, one has to look a gift horse in the mouth to be sure one can afford to feed it, much less pay taxes on it."

There was more, but Chalis was adamant. Her independence was vitally important to her at this point, and she could never justify accepting anything from a man whom she had come to despise. Oddly enough, after having made her decision almost without conscious thought, she was able to think of her late ex-husband with an abstract sort of pity. For almost two years he had made her life hell without once raising his voice. Most of his annihilating insults had been smilingly made, subtly designed to make her doubt her value as a person, and especially as a woman. Long after she had left him she had been plagued by those doubts. It had been those, and the desperate need to hide them, allied with the constant pressure of her job, of simply coping with the hectic pace of her life, that had brought her to a state of near collapse.

Only now, with the advantage of time and distance, had come the insight necessary to put her whole marriage in perspective. Jorge had staved off his own deep-seated insecurities by encouraging hers. He had found it necessary to purchase his self-esteem; she was fortunate enough to be able to earn hers. She still had her job—at least, she hoped she would after gently and tactfully rejecting Walt's proposal. Whatever happened, she had proved herself capable of making her own way. Never again would her ego be completely dependent on a man's opinion of her.

Lifting her head in an unconsciously regal attitude, she said, "Walt, I'm afraid I can't marry you."

His smile was little more than a rueful twist of the lips. "You're still upset, darling. I'm not at all sure that coming home was a good idea. These lotus-eating latitudes tend to undermine one's—"

"Lotus-eating latitudes?" she crowed disbelievingly. *"Davie County?"*

"We won't discuss it now, my dear, but I refuse to

take no for an answer. You've been overwrought these past few months, but basically you're still a sensible woman. There's no reason on earth why we shouldn't marry and every reason why we should. We'll just give it a bit more time."

She gave up. She knew Walt in this mood. A demolition derby couldn't break through that one-track mind of his!

A sensible woman! Swallowing her chagrin, Chalis decided that the ego she had so recently salvaged was still basically sound. So much for my rôle as a breaker of hearts, she mused.

Tackling him on familiar ground, she suggested farming out his new discovery—*if* they managed to land the artist. She wasn't too sure that L. Maurice wasn't already spoken for. Walt might believe civilization ended on the north side of the Mason-Dixon Line, but she had an idea L. Maurice was not going to be quite so easy a proposition as he imagined.

"We could do a private showing. The Lendermans would be a good possibility. They have plenty of room, and Neva's just done their whole place over. They'd love a good excuse for a soirée."

When Chalis stood to go, Walt was already scribbling notes and reaching for the phone. He had forgotten her presence before she had even left the room.

Chalis wandered out through the maze of ragged boxwoods to discover an overgrown rose garden that was half shaded by an enormous magnolia tree. The rumble of distant thunder disguised Benjamin's approach as she stood silently, her head thrown back and her eyes closed while she allowed the damp, spicy earthiness to seep into her limbs. A cat's paw of wind pressed her skirt against her thighs and feathered a few strands of glistening hair across one slightly flushed cheekbone.

"Admiring my gardening skills?" he asked her, coming to stand beside her. His deep drawl triggered a physical response which she deliberately made an effort to subdue.

"Admiring your lack of them," she admitted. She caught a whiff of that same muskiness that had clung to his shirt earlier, even though he had changed before lunch. Her nose must have registered the reaction.

"Sorry about that. I guess you've come a long way from the barnyard," he observed dryly.

She could hardly tell him that far from being repelled, she found the scent that clung to his clothing wildly disturbing. "Try me. I can ride any cow in your pasture," he grinned.

"You're on."

They took the truck, crossing several cattle guards as they headed for one of the long wood and metal outbuildings a quarter of a mile from the house. Halfway there, he pulled up and pointed to a small paddock where three yearling bulls grazed peacefully. "My future begetters."

At her questioning look, he continued. "Two of my best herd bulls are getting on toward retirement. Baltimore's ten this year, and as the song goes, he's too old to cut the mustard anymore. I have eight more in service now, ranging in age from four to nine, and these three fellows will be coming into their own in a couple of years."

She admired the sleek, brawny animals, their coats gleaming darkly in the brassy glare of a hazy sun. "Don't they fight?"

His grin flashed at her quickly as he rested a deeply tanned arm on top of the steering wheel. "So far they don't know what it is they have to fight over. Once I give each one of them his own harem, it'll be a different story."

As they neared the barn, Chalis inhaled the familiar sweet, pungent scent that had been so dear to her as a child. "Do you have any barn cats?" she asked suddenly, recalling one of her favorite things about her grandfather's farm.

"I wouldn't be surprised. We'll run over to the hay barn after a while and take a look, but first I thought I'd show you the new love of my life."

They passed several empty stalls before he paused at a whitewashed gate. "Buffy," he murmured, his voice warm with an emotion that caught almost painfully at Chalis's throat.

A golden head emerged above the gate, and Chalis stepped back to admire the beautiful palomino mare. "She's exquisite!"

"My sick friend," Benjamin elaborated. "Wait'll you see the love of *her* life. Come on, girl, move aside for us. That's right."

"A grulla gray," Chalis exclaimed, reaching out to touch the foal. "Oh, Ben, I envy you so. She's stunning. Look at that star!"

The foal was still at the fearless stage. Under the

golden quarter horse's watchful eye, Chalis was allowed to stroke the velvety nose, to tug gently at the comically large ears, and she allowed her finger to be sucked on before Benjamin drew her away. "She's not but a few hours old, so maybe we'd better come back later during visiting hours. That's what I was doing last night. It was Buffy's first, and she took a lot longer than usual. I started checking her every half hour after I got home last night. All systems were go, but nothing went until about five this morning. For breakfast, the vet and I broke out some champagne and drank a toast to our little girl."

The two champagne glasses in the library. "You must be dead! When did you sleep?"

"In the words of Scarlett O'Hara, I'll worry about that tomorrow."

"In the words of Chalis Kenyon, you'd darned well better take a break before you drive us to meet your friend tonight. I value my neck, even if you don't yours!"

His hand came around her neck, kneading the nape with strong fingers. "Oh, I value your neck, too, honeylove. Since you insist, we'll head for the hay barn and—"

"We'll head for the house! In fact, why don't you give me instructions to this studio and I'll take Walt, and you can get some sleep while we talk business."

At the door of the truck, he paused, bending over to rest his forehead on her shoulder. Chalis resisted an almost overpowering impulse to wrap her arms around him and hold him there, to run her fingers through that gleaming mahogany hair with its light frosting of silver. She allowed her cheek to brush briefly against its vital softness, then stepped back, firmly bracing him away from her. "You see? You're out on your feet."

"The haystack?" he suggested provocatively.

"The bedroom!"

"Better and better." He leered, and she turned him forcefully toward the driver's side of the pickup.

"Quit making indecent propositions and get us back to the house before you keel over," she laughed, swinging herself up into the high cab unaided.

Benjamin switched on the engine. "Did you let him down easy?"

She shot him a suspicious look. "I don't know what you—"

"Sure you do. You could no more marry that upholstered robot than—"

"Walt is *not* an upholstered robot! He's an extremely kind, extremely intelligent and cultured man, and I'm—"

"Extremely fond of him," Benjamin interrupted as they clattered over a cattle guard. "Sure you are. I'm extremely fond of smoked oysters and Godiva chocolates, too, but that doesn't mean I want a steady diet of them."

Settling herself into the corner of the cab, Chalis crossed her arms indignantly over her chest. Walt was *not*— Well, perhaps he was, just a bit. But that didn't excuse Benjamin's scathing attitude! She fumed until they pulled up beside the house, refusing to turn her head even when she felt Benjamin's mocking glance on her. *Smoked oysters and Godiva chocolates?* Her stern disapproval wavered under an unwelcome surge of amusement, and she pursed her lips and frowned determinedly.

"Sulking?" The soft rasp of his voice threaded through the humid stillness.

"Don't be ridiculous." She adopted her loftiest tone.

"Come wake me up at six. We'll allow about half an hour for you to do a thorough job of it, and then I'll drive you out to Quarter Moon and wait while you change into something fetching. I warn you, Lara takes some competing with." His glance was an undisguised taunt, even in his sleepless, red-eyed state.

"Whatever gave you the idea I'm competing? Walt's interest in her is purely professional, and anyway, Walt and I are merely business associates. . . . And very good friends," she added deliberately, echoing his own earlier emphasis.

He threw back his head and laughed, baring the strong column of his tanned throat, and Chalis glared at him in frustration before dropping down from the truck.

"Six o'clock!" he called after her as she marched stiffly toward the house.

"I'll drive myself back to Quarter Moon. I don't need your help!"

"Don't you, honeylove? I'm beginning to think maybe you do."

The afternoon extended into a sultry inferno. Chalis lingered at Yadkin Trace for the simple reason that it was several degrees cooler than Quarter Moon. With Benjamin asleep she felt secure enough, and she drew Walt out to the shaded rose garden, to a wrought-iron table and benches that felt almost cool to the touch. Pearl, a tiny, red-faced, gray-haired woman, who was built like a fire plug, served them weak iced tea and limp, store-bought cookies and disappeared into the house again.

The table was soon littered with notes as Walt made plans to launch his latest discovery.

"Walt, don't you think it might be wise to wait until after you talk to her? I mean, we don't know a thing about her, but she's certainly no Sunday painter. What if she's not interested?"

"In a New York exhibit?" he asked incredulously. "Don't be stupid!"

"But what if she's already signed with someone else? Walt, be reasonable. New York isn't the only city in the world, nor is Corticelli's the only gallery."

Walt discounted her reservations. One of the reasons they worked so well as a team was that Chalis's hard-won skepticism served as a balance for Walt's single-minded enthusiasms.

At five, Walt declared himself exhausted. "Why don't we go somewhere for a cocktail. I feel the need to breathe a bit of artificial air. All this wholesomeness can't be healthy."

Chalis was exhausted, too. The weather was at its most debilitating; a relentless sun still burned down on them, while over to the west, seething gray clouds mounted higher with a feckless promise of relief.

"I have a better idea. Let's go inside and I'll see if

Pearl will make us something long and icy. We can lie back under one of those ceiling fans and I'll tell you about the last time I went tubing down the Yadkin."

At six she left Walt listening to the news on television. Benjamin was awake—she could hear the sound of slamming drawers coming from somewhere in the house.

"I'll be back by seven. Ben says Miss Maurice's studio is about half an hour's drive from here, so we should make it in plenty of time. See you later."

Walt lifted a lethargic hand without turning his head, and Chalis let herself out, wondering how she could even have considered marrying him. Just as she shut her car door and switched on the ignition, she thought she heard Benjamin's voice. She ignored it and drove off. On the whole, she felt pretty proud of herself, and for a little while she wanted to savor the sense of accomplishment all alone. There was still the thing with Walt to settle, but she had made up her mind. That was the major part of the battle, and if she handled it well, she'd end up with her job intact, too. As for Jorge's estate, that could be managed by the lawyers, with her part no more than a signature or two.

So! Here she was: twenty-nine, solvent, in perfect health, and her entire future was in her own capable hands. There was a pleasant sensation of expectancy simmering just under the surface of her consciousness, as if she had tapped into the electricity in the very atmosphere.

Humming off-key, she let herself into the gate and drove down the winding road to the cabin. Tonight she would wear the new polished cotton, with its bold poppy print and the low square neckline. It was long, but it was sleeveless, backless and flowing—comfortable enough even for this sweltering weather. Here's hoping Lara Maurice's studio would be air-conditioned.

Oh, for a kerosene model blow-dryer! Careful not to wet her hair, she stood waist-deep in the soft, clear water and lathered herself with the fragrant soap. They had always used biodegradable products in the pond, and she watched the bubbles drift away from her slender, naked form and disintegrate. It was already quite dark because of the approaching squall, and across the pond the paler green trees gleamed with a fluorescent brilliance against the slate-dark sky. There were frequent flashes of lightning now; she'd better rinse herself off and get out of the water. While her knowledge of physics was sketchy at best, she had an idea an open pond wasn't the healthiest place to be, under the circumstances.

As she emerged from the water all her senses seemed somehow intensified. Head thrown back, she breathed deeply, relishing the feel of the cool shimmers of wind against her wetly gleaming skin, the dusty scent of the first raindrops striking the hot, parched earth. She almost regretted having to dress and drive the few miles back to Yadkin Trace. It might be years before she'd be able to feel this marvelous sensation of freedom, of—of glittering expectancy.

"My God, Chalis, do you have to do that?"

It was Benjamin! His dark figure separated itself from the shelter of the scarred oak and moved toward her, and she froze, totally unconscious of the nacreous gleam of her naked body. "Benjamin, what's wrong? What are you doing here? Where's Walt?"

For a frozen moment, both of them simply stood there. Every cell in her body was aware of Benjamin's eyes on her, and her physiological response was electrifying. It was as if she had known subliminally that he'd be here, known he'd find her like this. A flash of lightning illuminated his face, lending an unaccustomed harshness to his strong features.

"Get in the house," he grated. When she didn't move, he reached out for her, propelling her under the wide eaves just as the bottom dropped out. "God, I'm drenched already! How is it that whenever I'm out here with you, I always end up wet?"

They collided in the doorway and Chalis padded a few feet inside the stuffy, dark room, grateful that she hadn't lit the lantern before she bathed. Behind her, she was aware of movement, and then came the clink as Benjamin's brass buckle struck the floor.

"Benjamin, what are you doing?" She groped for a towel and found hard, wet flesh, instead. "Get out of my way, will you?"

Biting fingers came down on her shoulders, and he moved her aside. "I'm getting rid of these wet clothes! In case you hadn't noticed, the temperature's dropped ten degrees in the past few minutes, and not even for the sake of your maidenly modesty am I going to sit around and catch pneumonia while I wait for it to slack off!"

The words were all very reasonable. One part of Chalis's mind accepted them as common sense, but another part—the part that had been winding up tighter and tighter all day long—was totally conscious of the shimmering tension that thrummed through the small confined space—a space made even more confining by the furies that raged outside.

With a sense of inevitability, Chalis waited. It was as if every step she had taken from the moment she stepped on the plane at LaGuardia had led her to this point in time, to this place . . . to this man.

Benjamin had told her that he couldn't assume the responsibility, implied that he didn't want to get involved. Neither did she. Oh, Lord, that was the very last thing she wanted now that she had finally got herself on level ground again. So why was she standing here like a pillar of salt?

He touched her again then, his unsteady hands clamping onto her upper arms to shake her slightly, as if the turbulence outside had its counterpart inside him. With a sigh of something akin to relief, Chalis leaned against him, her forehead settling into the hollow of his shoulder, and he echoed her sigh as his hands slid down her back, sloping over the curve of her buttocks to lift her to him.

Chalis caught her breath as he brought her against his aroused body. A shaft of uncertainty stabbed through her as the memory of his recent rejection burned painfully into her consciousness; but at the solid warmth of his body, the reassuring circle of his arms, she relaxed.

Relaxed, that is, until the hammering of their two hearts, the thrust of his masculine body against her sleek, wet thighs, sent wild honey gushing through her veins. The feel of his chest pelt brushing against the tips of her breasts was unbelievably erotic.

Outside, lightning flashed almost constantly, while in the rich brown gloom of the cabin, lightning of another sort flashed between the two people who stood entwined in the middle of the room. Chalis felt the compulsion of the heavy sweetness begin to press the breath from her body, to drive the very life force in her on a relentless downward course. Her hips moved instinctively, and she felt the probe of Benjamin's instant response against her trembling thighs.

"Ahh, darling girl . . ." The words were soft explosions of pure feeling as he captured her face between his hands. Her arms wrapped around his waist, holding him to her as she waited with shuddering desperation for him to kiss her. His heart was thundering against her, his breath a ragged sweetness on her face. His lips hovered for an eternity, as if he still sought the will to resist, to hold back the inevitable forces. And then he surrendered, claiming her mouth with a soul-scourging intensity.

Without knowing how it came about, Chalis found herself lying on the narrow bunk with Benjamin half beside her, half on top of her. A fierce trembling shook his whole body as he struggled to wrest control from the primitive whirlwind that had gathered them both to its turbulent vortex. Her hand inched slowly over his shoulder to tuck itself into the secret crevass beneath his powerfully muscled arm, and she worked her fingers into the incredibly silky hair.

He jerked away, catching his breath. "You're

blowing on a dangerously short fuse, my water witch."

Intoxicated with a totally unexpected feeling of power, heady with a newfound sense of her own womanhood, Chalis allowed her fingers to tiptoe down his side to the hard narrowing of his waist. His body jerked with every touch of a finger on a rib, but he remained silent, and the very silence, the tightly harnessed passion, excited her immeasurably. Her hand moved again, her long, slender fingers reaching across his taut flesh to the flattened curls that surrounded his navel, and she felt the trembling of his abdominal muscles. Satiny, velvety skin covered hard, vital sinews. . . .

"Chalis, Chalis," he agonized, "do you know what you're doing?"

"I don't want to talk about it," she breathed. "I don't want to *think.*" Her lips formed the words against the slightly salty skin of his neck. Her tongue darted out to rake the hollow at the base of his throat, and suddenly she found herself bearing the full weight of his body. His mouth came down with hungry accuracy on the tautened nipple of one breast, and at the rasp of his tongue, the unbelievably sensuous feel of his eager mouth, her pelvis moved convulsively. His hand captured the thunder of her heart by shaping the soft mound of her other breast, and then it moved slowly downward to yet another heart, the heart of her womanhood, where a gathering storm of sensation spiraled higher and higher with shuddering sweetness.

Her fingernails raked over the skin of his buttocks, finding curious pleasure in the line of demarcation where the hair on his thighs began. Her palm flattened to slide to the inner side of his thigh, instinctively seeking the source of heat.

"You're killing me!" he moaned, adjusting his body to accommodate her explorations.

Thunder rattled incessantly, and the rain was a deafening drone, obliterating all thought, all reason. There was only Benjamin, only this powerful magnetic force field that held them both in thrall. Hopelessly lost in the rush of desire that pulsed through her, Chalis instinctively began to move in the age-old rhythm, blindly inviting Benjamin to join her in the dance of love.

And still he held back!

"Benjamin, don't you want me?" Her voice was a plaintive thread against the raspy sound of their tortured breaths.

He collapsed on top of her, burying his face in the damp tendrils of her hair. "Want you! Oh, God, Chalis, you can't be that naïve! I just want it to be good for you, darling. That means more to me than . . ." His voice trailed off as her hands began to move over his body with insatiable curiosity.

Benjamin captured her wrists in one of his hands and held them over her head. His eyes penetrated the darkness to the faint gleam of her slender body. Oh, God, she was so beautiful—and so terribly, terribly vulnerable! The timing was wrong, it was too soon, but there was no way he could stop it from happening. If only there had been more time to gain her trust. . . .

"Chalis, Chalis." His voice sounded raw, unrecognizable to his own ears.

His lips moved restlessly over her cheek, sliding over the delicate hollows that were so incredibly lovely. He tasted the slight soapiness on her neck, and then he was drawn inexorably to her small, perfect breasts. What he felt for her was all mixed up in the past and the future, and he had no business taking her now—not when she was still so close to the edge. She was over the worst of it. It was there in her eyes, in the way she laughed spontaneously now, the way she moved with an unconscious dignity that reflected her innate pride in herself as a woman.

His lips moved down her body, savoring the sweet generosity that allowed him his freedom. She had been all locked up inside herself before, as if she'd been afraid of letting go, afraid to live. Almost thirty, and God, she didn't even know what it was all about! That bastard had a lot to answer for.

He felt her fingers moving in his hair, then on his shoulders, raking a convulsive pattern that signaled her readiness. But first . . .

He pleasured her, using all the skill at his command, fighting against her own unschooled eagerness. It was important to him. Never mind just why, he'd deal with that later. For now, she needed to know how very desirable she was, how impossible it would be for her to tie herself up to—

"Oh, Benjamin, please—help me, help me!" The tiny, breathless sounds were all but lost in the thunder of rain on the metal roof, but he heard, he felt. He came into her then, awed by the timeless miracle of it all. Trembling with the effort, he held back until she moved convulsively beneath him, and then, helpless before the inevitable, he slipped over the edge and was lost.

He had wanted to go slowly, wanted it to be so perfect for her, but Christ! He hadn't counted on this! Shaken by a depth of feeling that went fathoms beyond mere sexual desire, he gave into the irreversible tides, and when he felt her clasping him in fierce, joyful waves, he raced to mount the highest wave of all, hovering on the crest for breathless, shuddering moments before coasting, spent, to the slack waters beyond.

Slowly, with ineffable sweetness, they drifted up through a warm and golden haze, both beyond words, beyond coherent thought. Outside, the thunder grumbled off eastward, flinging a last fitful scattering of rain behind it.

9

If, if, if! Chalis dashed barefooted through the tall, wet grass and climbed into Benjamin's car unaided. *If* he had not followed her here—*if* she had been all dressed and packed and ready to go—*if* she had had the good sense not to succumb to a moment's insanity brought about by propinquity and an unstable barometer!

"I'll come back in the morning and pick up anything you've forgotten," Benjamin said as he headed the car out the gate. He had driven a dark brown Seville instead of the usual pickup truck, and when Chalis had turned toward her agency car, he had steered her firmly away, mentioning the rain-flooded road into the property.

Chalis refused to look at him, but at that point she was too numb to put up more than a perfunctory objection. "The tornado alert will be long ended by morning. I'll come back here and stay," she announced flatly. She felt thrown together, decidedly at a disadvantage. To have to face Walt was going to be bad enough. To have to visit a "very good friend" of Benjamin's was beyond enough! "I still don't see why I can't come back here tonight. If a freak tornado does happen to come along, it could just as easily lift your roof off as mine."

But she knew that the devastation of a real tornado could hardly affect her more than the storm that had just passed.

It had been Chalis who had finally wrenched herself from Benjamin's arms to dash outside. He had come after her, and she had cried, "Good Lord, can't I have a minute's privacy? I'm not planning to throw myself in, you know!"

Benjamin had made an effort to reach her, but she had already turned inward, slamming the door securely on her devastated emotions. Neither of them had spoken further in the hectic few minutes it had taken to get dressed by candlelight. Unfortunately, both space and facilities were sadly lacking, and except for a few muttered curses on Chalis's part when she bumped into him inadvertently, and an increasingly baffled response on Benjamin's, he had given up.

What could there be to talk about? If he had the slightest idea how profoundly affected she was, he wouldn't expect her to be very chatty. If he had any idea what his lovemaking had done to her, what it had meant to her, he'd be three counties away and still running!

Keep it casual, he had said. He managed to keep

his affairs with women on a casual basis. Well, maybe one of these days she could treat sex with as much panache, but at the moment she felt as if the world as she had known it had just come to a blazing, fully orchestrated end!

By the time they pulled up at the Trace after a miserably silent drive, Chalis had managed to patch up a passable façade. Her social smile was plastered on, all ready for Walt when he came out to meet them.

"What happened to you? I thought you'd run into trouble. We're already twenty minutes late, and Miss Maurice called to see what was holding us up."

Thank goodness for the squall. It served as an excuse, and Chalis, after following Pearl upstairs to the guest room, took a few more minutes to do her hair and her makeup. She had no idea if she had the necessities for overnight. She had blindly slammed her suitcase shut back at the cabin, and Benjamin had snatched it from her hand and strode out to the car.

The evening inched by with tormenting slowness. Chalis made a conscious effort to fulfill her obligation as a guest, but it took almost superhuman resolution. She felt as off-balance as she had in the worst days of her marriage. How many times had Jorge allowed her to sparkle through an entire evening with a small, select gathering, only to shoot her down as soon as the door had closed behind the last guest?

If she had survived that, she could survive an evening of Lara Maurice's charming company, Walt's barely concealed avarice and Benjamin's baffled anger.

Lara had greeted them with disarming friendliness. Somewhere in her mid-thirties, she was one of the most attractive women Chalis had seen in a long time. While not precisely pretty, her animation and original style more than made up for any irregularity of features.

Benjamin had embraced her with a warmth that had left Chalis feeling strangely hollow. He had made the introductions, and from then on the evening had flowed before Chalis's numbed consciousness like a slow-motion film clip, starting with Lara's giving them all the grand tour of her studio. A combination of country charm and urban sophistication, the large, skylighted room was hung with her work as well as that of other artists. At any other time, Chalis would have been amused at Walt's reaction to the dozen or so large pastels done in the artist's highly individualistic style. He was practically salivating.

Chalis stood slightly aloof, observing, with no effort to interpret the interreactions of the other three people. Conversation flowed at a comfortable level. Some of the remarks actually came from her own stiff lips, but she had no idea what she said. She only hoped she didn't disgrace herself.

She smiled. Her eyes glittered feverishly, and she smiled and smiled and smiled, turning her head graciously at suitable intervals.

Dinner was a buffet of oddly assorted foods attractively served on hand-thrown pottery dishes, and Chalis rearranged them skillfully on her plate, ignoring the probing glances from Benjamin and the more speculative ones from her hostess. Walt waded through blintzes, stuffed grape leaves, fried okra, and cold shad roe with lemon with the same absent-minded omniverousness he had brought to Pearl's unpalatable offering.

After coffee and cognac, Lara said, "Ben, why don't you take Walt out and show him my raku kiln while I put these things away? Living and working in one room, even in one this large, has certain drawbacks. Chalis can keep me company—unless . . . ?"

Not especially interested in what she suspected might turn into a polite inquisition, Chalis nevertheless succumbed to an opportunity to escape Benjamin's watchful gaze. She was beginning to feel like a specimen under a microscope; if he thought she was about to fall apart just because he had made love to her a few hours ago, then he'd be sadly disappointed. She'd carry this thing off if it killed her!

Stapling her attention to the attractive artist, Chalis said, "Walt's impressed with you, in case you hadn't noticed."

Lara scooped up an almost empty tray of *dolmades* and carried them behind the storage wall that separated her minute kitchen from the open studio. "He's just a marshmallow under that fake British cool, isn't he? Or is it the other way around?" the tanned blonde in the linen burlap skirt and black silk shirt murmured. "Charming, though. I think we might be able to come to some arrangement, as long as he doesn't expect me to swear away my birthright."

Relaxing slightly, Chalis was unexpectedly amused. It had taken her five years to discover that Walt was as fallible as the next man under his expensively cultivated urban exterior. Lara had summed him up immediately and was completely on top of the situation. Nevertheless, Chalis felt compelled to warn her that Walt was a shrewd businessman, even when he was in hot pursuit of a "discovery"—*especially* then. "He's tough when it comes to contracts, but I suspect you're up to his weight."

"Until recently I exhibited at a gallery in L.A. It was run by a family of piranhas, but I managed to come out with a whole skin. I think I can look after myself. You see, my ace in the hole is that I really don't give a damn. I know I'm good. I don't need the money, and recognition doesn't mean a thing to me. As long as my work meets my own standards, then I'm happy, and that, after all, is what it's all about."

Chalis munched on a broiled mushroom cap filled with bacon and chicken liver. "He'll want fifty percent and the shipping is your problem."

"I'll give him the fifty. As I said, the money's no problem, but the shipping is his concern. Most of my work is still on the West Coast, and I don't want the hassle of dealing with it. Pastels are so damned delicate. Most shippers won't accept the responsibility, and even if they do, there's no such thing as a 'this side up' guarantee. Half the color ends up in a little heap at the bottom of the frame, because I refuse to use fixatives."

"Which explains that marvelous luminous quality you get," Chalis mused, her mind on the murmur of voices approaching from the backyard.

"Chalis—about Ben. Do I detect atmosphere between the two of you?"

Chalis sighed. She might have known those shrewd artist's eyes wouldn't miss the stiffness, the tension that stretched between herself and Benjamin like a crystalline thread.

The voices outside were diverted; they seemed to be sidetracked by something on the long sheltered porch which ran along one side of the main room.

"Yes—no—honestly, I'm not sure," Chalis sighed, leveling a slightly wary gaze at the older woman. There was no time to dissemble, even if she had the strength, and oddly enough, she discovered she liked Lara Maurice too much for anything less than honesty. Nevertheless, she was afraid of revealing too much. "Would it bother you if there were?"

Lara tossed the last dish carelessly into the dishwasher and slammed the door with a grimace. "That would depend on just what the situation was, wouldn't it?"

"I've known Benjamin for years," Chalis volunteered.

"Which tells me precisely nothing," Lara said dryly. "Want a drink?"

Chalis accepted a spritzer she didn't want and prepared herself for Lara's next move. She said, "I like your studio. Have you lived here long?"

"Translated, that means have I known Ben long. And the answer is that I've known him since just before his divorce from Jean was final. Trying to get close to him at that particular stage in his life was about like trying to get on friendly terms with a rabid hedgehog, but persistence won out. We've had a mutually gratifying relationship ever since, and I hope it will continue for a long, long time. If that tells you what you need to know, then I'm glad. I'm a bit past trading girlish confidences."

The two women eyed each other speculatively. Chalis called on every vestige of poise at her command to hide her dismay. She had the distinct feeling she had been kindly and politely warned off, and in spite of the fact that the warning was entirely superfluous, she resented it.

Resented it? She *hated* it! It took an almost superhuman effort on her part to saunter casually over to a delightfully uninhibited wall hanging and make some inane remark about it. It took slightly less to laugh when Lara told her she had bought it at a junior high school art show and had always been intensely jealous of the young artist who had created it with such a fine disregard of all rules of color and composition.

The men returned and Benjamin poured them both drinks. Chalis did not miss his easy familiarity with Lara's home. She finished her spritzer and held out her glass. "No soda this time, please."

Conversation skipped from topic to topic, but under Walt's determined direction, always returned to the subject of Lara's art. Chalis grew increasingly ill at ease as she felt both Lara's and Benjamin's eyes on her. From her hostess she sensed a sympathy she hotly rejected. It had been a mistake to lower her guard, even for a moment. Benjamin's attention was less easily interpreted. One moment he seemed brisk and animated, the next he was almost morose. It was as if a cloud had shadowed his hazel eyes, blocking his thoughts from her.

As a cover for her own growing despair, she drank

more than usual and slipped back into the brittle persona she had taken refuge in so often before. Turning to Walt with an animation that was utterly false, she felt Benjamin's eyes boring into her naked back. She leaned forward to place her glass on the coffee table and her fingers slipped on the wet crystal. The glass shattered against a large decorative geode, and as the tiny bit of wine remaining in it flowed across the polished surface, her spurious gaiety deserted her.

Lifting her large brown eyes apologetically to her hostess, she encountered instead Benjamin's enigmatic gaze, and then he was rising, making their excuses. "We've stayed too late as it is, Lara. I was up all last night with Buffy. By the way, it's a girl. Come out one day soon and pay your respects."

The ride back to Yadkin Trace seemed interminable—as endless as was the whole evening. Time was focused on a brief span at Quarter Moon Pond, and all that surrounded it seemed to Chalis to drift insubstantially through her consciousness like shadows of yesterday.

She went immediately to the room Pearl had shown her earlier, wishing she had the nerve to throw her things into her car and take off. It was only a few minutes after eleven, but she was dead on her feet. She'd probably end up in a culvert somewhere if she tried to escape.

"Damn," she swore softly as she remembered that her car was tucked away under the pines back at Quarter Moon. Her brain must have atrophied. She'd be forced to have someone drive her back in the morning, and that someone would undoubtedly be Benjamin! And there would be a carefully staged discussion in which both of them would utter politely worded lines, cautiously disclaiming any responsibility for what had happened.

She could imagine Benjamin's sickening cheerfulness: "Well, Chalis, I've enjoyed seeing you again after all these years. I guess you'll be headed north pretty soon. I probably won't see you before you go; got my hands full waxing the barn floor and painting the brood stock. It's been great fun, though—don't think it hasn't."

And she'd be just as bad. Her lips stretching in a ghastly grimace that was supposed to cover the gaping wounds in her psyche, she'd blather something idiotic about the fishing or the weather, and then he'd drive off and she'd cry, and then she'd kick something hard . . . something *very* hard! Oh, yes, she could see it all now.

Bitterness gave way to despair as she struggled to hold back the knowledge of just what had happened to her. She didn't bother to try and convince herself that it was only the sex. That had been shattering enough. Beautiful, wonderful, terrifying—all the words she had ever read to describe it fell far short.

And that was where the danger lay. Sex with Jorge had been an embarrassing little episode to be gotten through as quickly and as infrequently as possible. She had always felt vaguely like apologizing to him after it was over.

And now—Good Lord! What if she discovered she couldn't do without it? What if she became addicted? There was a name for that sort of unfortunate woman.

As the effects of the wine wore off, leaving her more depressed and confused than ever, Chalis paced the darkly gleaming wooden floor of her bedroom, pausing to stare out through the French windows. The clouds had moved on. Stars glittered in cold, innocent splendor.

"Where were you when I needed you?" she demanded, glaring up into the wedges of clear sky framed between the branches of a mimosa tree. The answering silence mocked her, mocked the sure knowledge that uncoiled inside her to fill her with a sense of hopelessness. It wasn't the fact that she had slept with Benjamin—God, what a euphemism!—it was the fact that she was in love with him. It had been creeping up on her for days—for years, probably—the same pure bright flame of idealistic passion she had nurtured as a girl before reality had extinguished it.

Only now it was magnified a thousandfold. Now, it meant far more than watching him from a distance. Now, it meant laughing with him, holding him, arguing absurd points with him. It meant sharing food with him, sharing ideas with him, simply knowing he was there to touch—warm, solid, gentle and strong.

She bit off a sound that was part sigh, part oath. There was no point in conducting a postmortem. What had happened had simply happened: no big deal for him; an earth-trembling revelation for her. But she'd handle it, just as she had handled every other crisis in her life, only perhaps with a bit more skill this time. Ironically, she felt stronger than she had in years. Even knowing she was going to have one hell of a time fleshing out the bare bones of her existence after tonight, she felt somehow whole, complete.

For perhaps ten minutes she stood under a rush of hot water and allowed it to wash away the dregs of the wine. Stepping out of the shower, she blotted herself absentmindedly and dug into her suitcase for her peach silk kimono, forcing herself to focus on what was to be done next. She should have discussed plans with Walt. He'd be leaving tomorrow, and if she hadn't been so almighty independent, she could have been gone as well. Instead, she'd have to wait until she could get a reservation.

Unless . . . perhaps it was still not too late. Crossing to the door of her room, she opened it slightly and peered out. Except for a nightlight in the hall, it was black as pitch. She rather thought Walt and Benjamin had lingered downstairs for a nightcap, but she couldn't be sure. She had been in such an all-fired rush to escape.

At any rate, they'd be finished and in bed by now. She had been pacing like a caged lioness for hours, it seemed. By now Benjamin would be out like a light, especially after last night's maternity watch in the barn.

Hoping she wouldn't blunder into something and wake the dead, she made her silent way downstairs. There was bound to be a phone somewhere on the second floor, but it would be just her luck to open the wrong door and find herself in Benjamin's bedroom. She could do without that!

A faint fluorescent glow from a kitchen appliance lit her way back toward the library, and she reached the door with no mishap. For the sake of privacy, she automatically closed it behind her, hoping she remembered exactly where the light switch was.

The room flared into brightness a second before her hand touched the switch. She caught her breath and sagged at the sight of Benjamin's looming form beside the leather-topped desk. One of his hands was on a brass and pewter lamp, the other wrapped around a whiskey glass, and he was weaving slightly even as she regained her own equilibrium.

Staring, she began to back away, but it was too late. Moving with fluid swiftness, he planted himself before her, one arm reaching out to brace against the closed door. "Were you looking for me, Chalis?" The rasping drawl was more pronounced than ever, the words slurred ever so slightly, and Chalis wondered if it was tiredness or the whiskey he had consumed.

"I thought you'd be in bed by now."

"Did you?" The mocking gleam in his eyes impaled her as if she were a helplessly fluttering moth. "Is that what you're doing here? You hopped into Poppa Bear's bed and found yourself all-l-l alone and lonely?"

"Don't be coarse!" Her heart was thundering under her weightless silk wrap, and she felt behind her for the doorknob.

"Coarse. Ahhh—so that's it! I wondered what had you all twisted out of shape." Leaning over, he placed his glass on the table and lurched slightly in regaining his balance. Chalis tried to take advantage of his momentary weakness to escape, but he caught her and jerked her against him. Her eyes flew to his mouth, seeing the derisive twist which failed to obscure the sensual fullness of his bottom lip. Tearing her eyes away, she blundered headlong into his heavy-lidded stare, and once more she dragged her gaze away.

"Coarse?" he repeated, and the slightly wounded note in his voice homed in unerringly on a weakness in her defenses. Lord knows, she was riddled with them, and every time he touched her he uncovered still more.

"The princess and the peasant. . . . Hear ye, hear ye! Lady Chalis committed the unpardonable sin of making love with one of the lower orders." His arms were crushing her against him, his chin burrowing into her scalp so hard it hurt. "Tell me, my fastidious darlin', did the smell of the barnyard linger on your alabaster skin?" He had trouble with the word alabaster. "Are you afraid that overstuffed toy you're planning to marry might be offended if he sus-suspected you of a tumble in the hay with th' resident hayseed?"

She twisted her head away, leaning back in his arms to glare up at him, but at the thought of what he might read in her eyes, she lowered her face in defeat. Ironically, the very fact that he had found it necessary to drink too much, whether from bitterness or some obscure feeling of inadequacy—although, Lord knows, he was anything but that—made him seem unexpectedly vulnerable.

And that she couldn't handle. An insolent, scornful Benjamin she could have dispatched with little effort. A swaggering Benjamin who blatantly crowed over his conquests—that she could have dealt with swiftly and effectively. At least, she sincerely hoped she could; bruised pride and righteous indignation were relatively easy forms of defense.

But this other Benjamin, this creature who held her as if she were about to melt and flow through his fingers, this man who gazed down at her so hungrily as he swayed with a combination of drink and exhaustion; she had no defenses at all against him.

"Benjamin, let me go. You should have been asleep hours ago."

"Couldn't sleep. Listened to that pontificatin' bastard friend of yours until I couldn't take it anymore, an' I came in here to get myself a stiff drink. Had two, for good measure." He grinned down at her and her hand lifted helplessly to stroke his bristly, belligerent jaw.

"Oh, Benjamin, somebody needs to pour you into bed, and I don't think I can manage it. Is Pearl—?" She glanced vaguely around. There was no one at all in this wing. "No, not Pearl," she muttered, dismissing the tiny housekeeper who'd be snoring in her own quarters by now.

"Never fear, ol' Benjamin's here! I'll help you. The two of us can han'le me, don' you think?" he asked lugubriously. The slur had become noticeably worse in the few minutes she had been in the room.

"No, I don't think! Dragging you up those stairs would be about like trying to waltz with a buffalo!" She laughed and it sounded remarkably like a sob. A feeling of inevitability swept over her as she attempted to support him, and instead of his leaning on her, somehow she found herself reaching around his boneless torso to hold him against her side.

"The couch, then. Maybe we can make it tha' far. Jus' drop me an' go to bed, honey . . . I'll be fine, jus' fine." His head came down again on top of hers, and his deep, regular breathing stirred the flyaway strands of her hair. His whiskey-scented breath flowed warmly about her, and she closed her eyes despairingly against the overwhelming force of the love that racked her.

It was hopeless! She loved him hot and warm from the sun, smelling of horses and cattle, and she loved him dressed in lean white linen slacks and a brown silk shirt as he moved familiarly about another woman's home. She loved the feel of him inside her, on top of her, surrounding her as he cried out his joy in fulfillment; and she loved him like this, shirt awry, hair awry, smelling of bourbon and out on his feet.

Together, they made their unsteady way across the dimly lit room to the long, leather-covered sofa. Chalis braced her legs against the edge and prepared to guide Benjamin's heavy weight so that he fell in more or less a horizontal position. Instead, he lowered himself onto the cushions and pulled her down on top of him.

"Benjamin—let me up!" she sputtered, elbowing his chest.

He dealt swiftly and effectively with her opposition by brushing her elbows outward so that she collapsed in a heap, her legs tangled with his and her face buried in the open front of his shirt. "Benjamin!" she gasped impotently.

His recovery was nothing short of miraculous. One hand stroked down her back, pressing her tightly to the length of him as he grinned lazily up into her outraged face. She glared at him, and when the strain of supporting her head became too much for her, he tugged it down into the hollow of his shoulder.

"There, there, honeylove, don't carry on so fiercely. I'm not going to hurt you. I wouldn't hurt you for the world," he rumbled against her ear.

For a while he was silent, with only the heavy sound of his breathing rending the late-night stillness. Had he fallen asleep? Was it possible? Oh, God, *anything* was possible! She had certainly proved that with her own erratic, insane behavior.

And then he came alive. His hands were everywhere: in her hair, twisting to angle her head to receive his kiss; on her back, pressing her thrillingly against his quickening body. He brought her head down so that her mouth covered his and she stubbornly kept her lips clamped shut.

"Open for me, damn you," he growled, tugging her chin. No sign of the inebriated slurring now, his voice rasped tersely as he ordered her to kiss him. "Kiss me as though you meant it. Kiss me like you did before. There's a real, live woman living inside you, damn it, Chalis, and I want her to come out again!" His fingers slid between them to search for the knot of her sash.

"Chalis . . . please," he whispered against her mouth.

There it was—that pleading note again. As if it mattered to him. As if *she* mattered to him.

"Let me go, Benjamin," she begged, freeing

herself enough to turn her head away. The fight she was waging against him—oh, God, against *herself*—was taking its toll!

He captured her jaw again and attempted to force her lips apart, and when that failed, he hooked a finger over her bottom lip to probe her tightly clenched teeth. "You'll draw back a nub," she warned him, and then, to her utter consternation, she felt his body begin to shake beneath her. She stiffened suspiciously. "Benjamin, are you laughing?"

His gasps erupted then, the deep, uninhibited laughter she had come to love so much, and she was lost. "Oh, Benjamin," she wailed, and then she was laughing with him, and she hadn't the slightest idea why. Imperceptibly, laughing became crying, and she was sobbing against his neck, her tears joining his perspiration in a salty elixir, and he was holding her, murmuring comforting love words against her cheeks, her drenched eyes.

"Honeylove, my little white heron, my prickly little cactus, don't cry."

"I'm not crying," she blubbered, sniffling as she reached under his hips for his pocket handkerchief.

He shifted obligingly and the thrust of his pelvis against hers had an immediate effect. Scrubbing her face with the white linen square, she tried to ignore what was happening beneath her, tried to edge away from him, but it was no use. Benjamin's hand slipped down her back to hold her against him, rounding her buttocks with slow, savoring strokes, slithering the silken fabric against her skin until every nerve ending in her body was alight.

"Make love to me, darling," he commanded softly, guiding her so that she was seated astride him.

"No, Benjamin, please. I don't want this." Even as the words fell weakly from her lips, her body was moving, adjusting itself as her thighs clasped his sides in a sensual embrace. "No, Benjamin—no, no, no," she chanted. Her hands were working at the fastening of his beltless pants.

"Yes, my love, yes, yes, yes," he chorused. His own hands were busy on her shoulders, exploring the subtle hollows, the fragile bones, before sliding along her arms to carry the loose-fitting kimono down to a soft puddle of silk about her hips. His fingertips traced their way back up the sensitive inner side of her arms, brushing lightly over highly inflammable nerves before moving inward to tantalize her breasts. He brushed his flat palms slowly across the tumescent peaks, telegraphing frantic messages through her body.

"You're as lovely as a dream of moonlight, Chalis—like some unearthly ice princess come to torment me." His hands conjured a spell of body magic, revealing secrets that had been hidden from her all her life—hidden and waiting for a master magician to release them with the touch of his magic wand.

He continued to play lightly over her sensitized nerves until she was half crazed, and then, when she felt as if she'd explode from the scintillating tension that bonded them together like a surge of electricity, he lifted her and resettled her over him with exquisite slowness.

As if in a dream, Chalis found herself following his lead, mindlessly obedient to the slightest command of his masterful hands, until finally he handed over the reins and allowed her to set the pace. By then she had long since passed the point of no return, and under Benjamin's encouragement, his increasingly incoherent direction, she moved blindly along a course where the only guide was pure instinct—nor did that play her false.

Much later, Chalis lifted her head reluctantly from the hard pillow of his shoulder. Her cheek was wet, and she wasn't sure if it was from tears or exertion—probably both. She touched the tip of her tongue to Benjamin's throat and savored the salty taste of him. He didn't stir at all. His breath came in slow, even strokes, moving her whole body as she lay on top of him.

Cautiously, she sat up. He mumbled something under his breath, and she paused, one foot on the floor, but he didn't awaken.

"Benjamin?" She whispered his name tentatively. No reaction. The hours of missed sleep were telling on him now, in spite of the short nap earlier that afternoon. The level in the bottle on the desk was not appreciably lower than it had been when she and Walt had come in here after breakfast, so he couldn't have had all that much to drink.

God, had it only been that afternoon? Had she wandered into some strange new time zone, destined to hang in limbo forever?

The phone was on the desk, at the other end of the long, narrow room. Chalis stared at it until it blurred before her eyes. Her mind was only now creaking into action again, and she wished she had the nerve to finish off the bourbon Benjamin had left. Anything to hold back the time when she had to begin to think.

Drinking wouldn't help, though. There was no easy answer for what ailed her, but she had come too far along the road to recovery to turn back now. Moving slowly, Chalis rearranged Benjamin's clothes with lingering, loving care. She covered his sleeping form with the woven spread on the back of the couch and stared down at him for a long, long time before making her way silently to the phone.

She had forgotten how ineffably lovely daybreak in the country could be—and how very noisy. Standing beside the open window of her bedroom, Chalis watched the sun mount the top of the riverside trees, endowing hundreds of dew-wet spider webs with sunbursts of diamonds. A family of adolescent blue jays squabbled stridently over breakfast in the mimosa that brushed her balcony.

Numbly, she gazed down on Benjamin's head as he emerged from the side door to climb into the truck. She waited until he was past the second cattle guard on the way to the horse barn before going downstairs to call her uncle.

Forty-five minutes later, she was headed toward Quarter Moon in Leonard Kenyon's dependable sedan. "Care to talk about it, honey?" he prompted, but she shook her head in silent misery. All she had told him was that she needed a ride to Quarter Moon, and the sooner the better.

"I'll pick you up in an hour and a half," Chalis had told Walt. "That will give us plenty of time." He had nodded absently, checked his watch for the seventh time, and asked if she thought Lara would be awake by now.

Steffie and Leonard insisted on seeing them off. "I'm semiretired now, honey, and between Steffie and my doctor, I'm more tied down than ever. Let me get a vicarious thrill by watching other people take off for parts unknown, at least," her uncle had pleaded ruefully.

"New York City is hardly 'parts unknown,'" Chalis chided, wrapping her arm around her uncle's waist affectionately. "On second thought, maybe it is. Maybe I'll discover Dr. Livingston alive and well in darkest Central Park."

"You stay out of darkest Central Park," Leonard warned with mock severity. "You could always get a job back home, honey," the older man continued, with a searching look at her pale features. "I've still got a lot of contacts around these parts."

Chalis turned her head away to hide the sudden rush of longing that threatened her composure. She had crossed her fingers that Benjamin would still be out when she returned to collect Walt, and her luck had held. If she could only put him out of her mind until she settled into her job again, then she could deal with the pain later. Meanwhile, the warmth and concern in her uncle's eyes was going to do her in unless she got out of here quickly!

Chalis informed Walt it was time they went to the

boarding gate. It was early still, but since flights were not called, perhaps no one would notice.

They were saying final goodbyes at the glass doors of the barrier when the hair on Chalis's nape began prickling. With a sense of fatalism, she turned slowly to confront Benjamin across the busy expanse of the crowded waiting room. He was still breathing hard, evidently having run from the parking area to the terminal building, and at the accusing look in his eyes, she ducked her head and slid a kiss off her aunt's cheek. Turning to her uncle, she threw her arms around his neck and allowed the swelling pressure of love to overflow for an instant. As if he understood and accepted his surrogate rôle, the older man patted her comfortingly on the shoulder and murmured, "There, there, sweetheart; it's going to work out, just you wait and see."

Grabbing the bag of peaches and assorted home-made relishes her aunt had presented her with, she shoved against the swinging doors, presented herself for the security check and strode down the terrazzo corridor, not even looking to see if Walt was following.

He could hit her! He could cheerfully shake her until those elegant bones of hers rattled like seeds in a dried gourd!

Benjamin stood helplessly and watched the narrow back in the jade green linen dress disappear down the corridor with Gregory trotting along after her like a tame poodle. No, like a blasted Afghan—showy, expensive and inexpressibly stupid! Walt couldn't begin to understand a woman like Chalis, much less appreciate her. Much less make her happy.

"I'll give her a month," he muttered rawly as he stared through the glass-doored security barrier, "one month at the very most, and then I'm going after her."

10

It was good to be back in harness. It *was* good to be back! If she said it often enough, repeated it like a litany, perhaps she'd come to believe it.

But no self-inflicted pep talk seemed to change the fact that to Chalis's haunted eyes, the pervasive color of Manhattan was a depressing shade of gray, the prevalent sounds harsh and strident. Leaving home . . . no, not home! *This* was home. Still, leaving Davie County in mid-summer only made the contrast more marked.

Standing before her burgeoning filing cabinet, her fingers trapped between KNAPP, AVRIL JAMES and KNOTRESS AND CLINE: PUBLICISTS, her mind swept back along the familiar narrow, curving highway that ran past Quarter Moon, through the lovely little town of Clemmons, to Winston-Salem. A vision drifted into focus: Summer-laden trees rose dark and heavy, casting smoky blue shadows across lush meadows hemmed with blossoming blackberry vines. Here and there a small creek dawdled through the somnolent haze.

Ruthlessly, she pounced on her own sentimentality; that same idyllic scene could be found right here in New York State, or in any of the intervening states, she rationalized. After almost two weeks, it was time she shook it off. At this rate, she'd find herself right back under Dr. Adelburg's capable care.

"We're meeting the Townsends at one for lunch, Chalis. You haven't forgotten, have you?" Walt reminded her from the doorway.

Her smile reflected a large measure of frustration. Walt had asked her twice more to marry him, and when she tried to let him down diplomatically, he had turned conveniently deaf. She had no intention of lapsing into any lukewarm arrangement with him, but it looked as if she'd have to tackle him with a half nelson to force him to accept her rejection.

Lingering over coffee and cheese in one of Walt's favorite establishments that night, Chalis felt the color drain from her face.

"Chalis? Did you hear what I said?" Walt prompted. "What's wrong? Don't you feel well?"

Her shoulders sagged as disappointment shafted through her. It wasn't Benjamin. Just another tall, well-built man in an unobtrusively well-cut suit, with a way of carrying himself, a way of holding his dark, lightly frosted head, that reminded her of the man who was making such a mockery of all her efforts at rehabilitation.

It was the fourth or fifth time it had happened since she had fled from those angry, baffled eyes back at the airport. And it had to stop, she told herself despairingly. It was only another manifestation of her homesickness, after all. It was just a lingering infatuation aggravated by a dose of homegrown lust, but she'd soon be able to put it out of her mind, now that she was caught up in the excitement of work again.

She had been a real mess when she had gone running home last month. Given the proper perspective, it was easy to see that it hadn't been a matter of specifics so much as a generally run-down condition. It had taken only one more straw to break the proverbial camel's back, and there had been two of them: Jorge's unexpected legacy and Walt's proposal.

Once she had gotten off by herself she had rested, eaten like a horse, and tackled her problems with characteristic efficiency. The fact that she had yet to make Walt accept her answer was beside the point. More important was the fact that she had laid to rest the ghost of her marriage. Jorge had no power to hurt her anymore, and after an uncomfortable forty-five minutes of listening to old Mr. Smithson speaking in fine print, she had signed a few documents, given him the name of her tax accountant and walked out minus one more headache.

Walt ushered her out of the restaurant and into a light drizzle, hailed a cab and directed the driver to Chalis's apartment. He had been dropping laden remarks all evening, and now he picked up her hand and laced his fingers through hers in an unusual attack of demonstrativeness. "We need to talk, darling. I've been more than patient with you, but I'm only human, you know."

Chalis suppressed an embarrassing recollection of one of Benjamin's more unflattering descriptions of the man beside her. Walt was one of the nicest men she had ever known. He'd been there when she desperately needed someone, and she'd never forget it. Still, that wasn't any basis for marriage.

The phone was ringing as she entered her small, stylishly decorated living room. She dashed for it and lifted the receiver eagerly to her ear, only to hear the connection broken. With the phone humming impotently in her hand, she experienced a hollow certainty of who had been on the other end. In her mind's eye she pictured the phone on the desk in Benjamin's library, and as absurd as it was, her eyes shimmered wetly in frustration, and she turned her back as Walt joined her.

"Who is it?" he mouthed. "Chalis?" he prompted at her continued silence.

It was like cutting off an arm, to put down the receiver. As long as she held the line open, she was tenuously connected to Benjamin, to Yadkin Trace.

"Chalis, for God's sake, snap out of it!"

Biting off a sigh, she put down the phone and turned a brilliant smile on the man who hovered awkwardly beside her. She was doing it again! Capable, efficient, supposedly mature Chalis Kenyon was acting like a fourteen-year-old with her first crush.

Which was only fitting, under the circumstances, she acknowledged bitterly. "Walt, if you'd like a drink, help yourself. I seem to have collected a headache."

He eyed her searchingly, and wearily she began arming herself for another bout of frustration. "Walt—" she began.

"No, don't bother, Chalis. You'll be hiding out in the bathroom next. Sooner or later you're going to come to your senses and marry me." His cool, noncommittal eyes pinned her uncomfortably so that she couldn't look away. "Oh, I know you think you're in love with Poe—and don't look at me like that! I'm not the blind idiot you take me for, Chalis, but Poe's back there on the farm, and you're here where you belong, and quite frankly, my dearest, I can't see you milking cows and entering county fairs for the rest of your days." His gaze took in her oyster satin suit, with the black and brown chiffon blouse and the bronze T-strap shoes. Clustered pearl and topaz earrings were her only jewelry.

Resting her elbows against Walt's shoulders, Chalis leaned her forehead on his chest. Instead of laundry detergent and horses and tobacco, his shirt smelled of an expensive, custom-blended cologne, and she lifted her head again wearily. "Walt, I am a blind idiot. I admit it freely and frankly, but there's not much I can do about it. We both know it wouldn't work. I appreciate your asking me more than you know, but it's just no go," she said dully.

He was going to kiss her and she was too tired to argue. Following the line of least resistance, she lifted her face. There was nothing in any way unpleasant in his kiss. He had kissed her before, had even made a rather stilted effort at going a step further once or twice, but they had both been relieved when she had fielded his pass with a tactful evasion. Now, with the feel of his discreetly padded, mohair-covered shoulders under her fingers, and the cool pressure of his lips on her mouth, she willed herself not to remember another set of shoulders, another set of lips.

"Never mind, my dear, it'll come," he murmured, holding her head against his chest. His touch was carefully light, so as not to disturb her flawlessly styled hair, and irrationally, she resented it. "The physical side of marriage will work out well enough, but more important at our age and in our position, we know we're completely compatible. We've been friends as well as business associates—closer by far than if we'd merely had an affair. We'll have a good marriage, Chalis. We have the same interests, and that can only increase as time goes by. I promise you, my dear, you won't be sorry."

"Don't you ever *listen?*" she asked, exasperated at his unshakable ego. "Walt, I've told you over and over that I can't marry you! I even gave away my dowry, remember?" Was it her imagination, or did he actually wince at that reminder? "Walt, believe me, I like you enormously, but I'd make you a terrible wife."

"You're just tired, my dear. As for the collection, you did what you thought best, so why don't we both try to forget it? And now, it's late and I'm keeping you up. Take the morning off tomorrow. We don't have anything really pressing until eleven, do we? Tansey can cope."

After he had left, Chalis sat for a long time, her feet curled under her on the sofa. Her eyes moved around the small room, with its muted neutrals and white bamboo, the cabriole-legged dressing table of doubtful origin that served as a desk, and the handsome brass and glass étagère she had rescued from a bankruptcy sale at an obscure restaurant. All were enhanced by carefully placed overgrown houseplants, but suddenly, she felt a vague dissatisfaction with it all. It was too slick, too contrived. She much preferred a decor that evolved naturally over several generations of living.

The following afternoon she let herself into her apartment to hear the phone ringing again. Dropping her purse and her flat cordovan briefcase, she dashed for it and panted a breathless greeting.

"Chalis? It's Tansey." Her heart plunged to the soles of her gunmetal patent pumps. "You left too soon," the vivacious secretary declared. "Five minutes after you walked out the door, you got a call from an old flame."

"What old flame? Tansey, what are you raving about?"

"Would you believe Rhett Butler? No, wait—I'm serious! Even the sound of his voice asking for Miss Kenyon made me think of mint juleps and a four-poster bed strewn with magnolia blossoms."

"Tansey, quit sniffing correction fluid and be serious! Did he give a name? Was it—"

"Benjamin Poe. Biblical and literary, all at the same time. Chalis, I think I'll relocate. Do you think I could find me a Solomon Faulkner, maybe? Or how about a Jedediah Hemingway? I can see it all now: He'll take my arm when we come to a hole in the sidewalk just so I won't break a leg and have to be shot, and he'll hand me in and out of taxis as if I were just too, too fragile. Hell, he might even pay for me on the subway!"

"Tansey, we don't have subways where Ben and I come from," Chalis said dryly. "Now wake up and tell me exactly what he said. What did you say? Did you give him my address and phone number?"

"Do you think I'm batty? I can drool over the phone all I want to, but I know better than to hand out that kind of information to every guy with a brown velvet voice. For all I know, Jack the Ripper had a Southern drawl! And in case you're thinking of calling him—"

"That's what I'll do! Thanks, Ta—"

"He said he wasn't calling from home, but he didn't say where he was," the secretary announced flatly. Chalis thought she must be mistaken in thinking she heard a certain malicious smugness in the tone. She and Tansey got along beautifully.

Chalis expelled her exasperation in one long gust. After all, she was the one who had gotten the unlisted number after her divorce. Tansey was only following her instructions. "If he calls back—"

"Look, he already knows your home number—you probably gave it to him and forgot it—but he asked your address, and I started to give it to him, but I figured if you hadn't, I shouldn't, right? And I'm leaving as soon as I unplug the coffeepot. He'll probably get you tonight, or if not, he'll try again tomorrow."

Tomorrow was light-years away, and she wouldn't be here tonight! There was an interminable evening to be gotten through somehow. Walt had arranged to bring together one of his lesser-known artists and a notoriously difficult collector, and it was going to require all Chalis's social finesse.

By the time she had fallen into bed, she was exhausted to the eyebrows. The collector collected to compensate for a tragically deprived background and his subsequent sense of inferiority. The artist was inclined to be more egotistical than his current status warranted, and she had had a hard time neutralizing some of his more outrageous remarks. Still, that was what she was paid for. Fourteen hour days, six day weeks, and an unlikely knack for silk-glove refereeing.

She fell into bed at one-twenty, lay awake staring at the ivory bedside phone until after two, and overslept the next morning. It was raining hard, and she couldn't locate her umbrella. Just as she was leaving, the super called to announce a new policy on garbage pickup, and there wasn't a cab to be had.

"Just missed him," Tansey announced proudly when Chalis hurled herself through the door at ten-fifteen. "But don't worry, I didn't let him get off the hook this time."

Standing on Walt's antique Persian rug, Chalis shook out the few ounces of white nylon that served as a raincoat and glared impatiently at the secretary. "Well? *Well?*"

"You're to meet him for lunch at twelve-thirty." She named the address and handed Chalis the scrap of paper on which it was scribbled. "He said if you couldn't make it, that he'd understand. And Chalis, don't worry—if you've got something else lined up, I'd be glad to fill in for you. Self-sacrifice is my middle name."

"You mean he's here? Here in town? Are you sure he wasn't calling from North Carolina?"

Tansey shrugged her plump shoulders. "If he was, he's gonna have to do some fancy stepping to make it in time for lunch." She applied her nail file with suspect diligence. "You know, if I were you, I'd think twice about playing around with two men like Walt and this Benjamin guy. They're both keepers, and legally, you can't keep 'em both. Maybe you'd care to share the wealth?"

Chalis glanced at her impatiently. She was in no mood for games. "Oh, for Pete's sake, Tansey, don't be silly! You know I'm not going to marry Walt."

"Yes, but does *he* know it?"

"Well, if he doesn't, it's not my fault! What else can I do short of walking out on a perfectly good job?"

The younger woman held an index finger up to the light and examined it frowningly. "Hmmm—I'll have to get it mended."

Chalis strode into her office, her mind on anything but her perfectly good job. Benjamin was here! He had been here in town all along; she could have been with him all this time. Oh, damn and blast! She felt like howling.

Her office extension was buzzing and she picked it up, unable to concentrate on current shipping restrictions to a certain Middle Eastern country. If Mr. Shariz wanted his welded copper fountains anytime soon, he could just send his own private air force for them!

By noon she had changed her mind a dozen times. Phrases such as "clean break" and "cut your losses" found loopholes in her common sense and slipped away, to be replaced by a memory of shared laughter and mutual passion. She mislaid an important letter and snarled at Tansey until the thing turned up again where Chalis had left it the day before.

At twelve-fifteen she put on her raincoat and strode past Tansey's curious gaze. At least she didn't have to answer to Walt; he was meeting a man from a Palm Beach hotel about fielding a rotating exhibit there.

There was hardly even any breathing space between the raindrops, and the cabs had all been magically whisked away to that invisible plane where cabs existed when they were desperately needed. Finally Chalis spotted one cruising on the opposite side of the street. Jumping a muddy river, she tackled it and let herself in, blinking to decipher the rain-blurred address on the scrap of paper she had been clutching like a talisman.

Halfway there, her driver hooked bumpers with a limo bearing diplomatic plates. Chalis pitched forward to crack her forehead on the partition. She wasn't really hurt, but the driver of the limo insisted she remain until he could get a release for her to sign. Short of precipitating an international incident, there was nothing she could do. Helplessly, she watched the hands of her watch pass twelve-thirty and head inexorably upward. She could have wept. By the time she was free to go again, it was getting on toward two. Benjamin would have long since given up, thinking she didn't want to see him.

Driving back to the office, she brooded morosely on the vagaries of fate. A plump little man with a modified Dali mustache and an anxious accent had probably totally ruined the rest of her life!

Back at the gallery, she waited on tenterhooks for the phone to ring again. Surely Benjamin wouldn't just give up. He had called the gallery more than once and missed her. He had called the apartment . . . maybe. She had nothing except a finely tuned intuition to go on, but he could have easily gotten her number from Uncle Leonard. Oh, God, this was worse than her high school days, when she waited by the phone for hours, muttering incantations!

As her own devil's advocate, Chalis was unbeatable. Benjamin had called several times and missed her by a hair. He had said if she didn't show at the restaurant he'd understand.

Understand what? Chalis herself didn't understand what was going on. She only knew she was a blithering fool who didn't know when she was well off. If she had good sense, she'd snap up Walt and forget everything below the Mason-Dixon Line.

She was leaving for the day—one of the most miserable, nonproductive days she had spent in a long time—when Tansey stopped her with an over-casual query. "Missed your friend at lunch?"

"You know damned well I missed my friend at

lunch," Chalis snapped back. "I'm sorry, Tansey, it's not your fault. It must be this rain or something. Maybe I need to double up on my stress vitamins."

"Well, doubling up on men doesn't seem to be what you need, that's for sure. Since you can't seem to straighten yourself out, I decided to poke my oar in. I gave your address to Benjamin. And if you're upset with me, then go ahead and hit me, only for Pete's sake, do it and get it over with. I can't stand another day like today."

Chalis dashed out the door, ducked back inside and apologized to the baffled secretary, started out again, then came back inside. With a bemused smile on her face, she hurried to the lounge and dumped her purse out on the table, scrabbling for her makeup and a tiny hairbrush.

Ten minutes later she emerged to find the lights shut off except for the two small spots they used in the display window and the single fluorescent left on in Tansey's office to make the place look inhabited. Letting herself out once more, she locked the door behind her. The rain, thank goodness, had stopped, and now the atmosphere was like a greenhouse, quickly wilting her freshly done hair and makeup job.

What a comedy of errors! She'd die if Benjamin ever discovered how she had reacted to his calls and the frustration she had met at every turn. It occurred to her to wonder for the first time what he was doing here. She didn't flatter herself that he'd come this far just to see her. It must be business. Even farmers were allowed a few outside interests, and let's face it, Benjamin Poe was not an ordinary, run-of-the-mill farmer. Yadkin Trace reflected generations of money well spent, as well as a variety of interests beyond breeding registered Angus and keeping a few quarter horses.

She ran up the last two flights, key in hand, her imagination working overtime. Could that be her phone ringing? She was almost positive it was, and if she didn't reach it this time, there wouldn't be a second time—or a fourth!

"Hello, Chalis."

For long moments she stood there gaping like a goldfish. "Benjamin?" she croaked finally. "Benjamin, what are you doing here?" Her hand was extended, the key already aimed in the general direction of the lock, and he took it from her and calmly opened her door, ushering her inside before she could come to her senses and realize that he was actually here . . . in person.

And it *was* her phone ringing! In confusion, she gazed blankly at the shrilling instrument and then at Benjamin, and finally his mouth twisted in a quizzical grin. "I begin to understand why my calls go unanswered."

Snatching up the receiver, she squeaked a greeting of some sort. It was Tansey. "Did he get there? Is he there now? Does he look like he sounds? No, of course not. That sort never does. Probably wears Coke bottle lenses in clear plastic rims and has—"

"Tansey, for gosh sake, what do you want?" She was acutely aware of Benjamin's eyes moving over her, taking in every detail of her bedraggled appearance. It had been a rotten day and she felt ancient!

"When I decide to meddle, I don't fool around. Just wanted to be sure you two had finally made connections," the younger girl replied blithely before hanging up.

Chalis's shoulders lifted in a mystified sigh, and she dropped her raincoat, her briefcase and her purse to the floor. She was too spent even to put them away, and in a room the size of her living room, one unscheduled bud bursting into bloom could throw the whole place into confusion.

They stood facing each other, Chalis's arms hanging limply at her sides. Her mind was dithering hopelessly as her eyes clung to the green-gold gleam of Benjamin's. After an eternity he moved to close the distance between them. When his hands reached out toward her, Chalis instinctively leaned forward, but he only lifted a section of hair that had fallen damply to cling to her neck.

Wordlessly, she continued to stare at him. His hands moved to the gold filigree bar pin that closed her pink silk shirt at the neck, and he removed it. Then they dropped to the rose-colored kid belt, and he unfastened it and allowed it to fall to the floor. "Your shoes," he murmured. "Take them off."

In a state bordering shock—albeit a warm, bewildering sort of shock—she obeyed; and then, when she stood before him in her stocking feet, her blouse opened and her slate gray linen skirt wrinkled at the waist from the wide belt, he smiled at her. It was as if the sun had risen in the west.

Half mesmerized, she said, "Benjamin, would you mind telling me what the devil is going on here?"

"You look about like I feel—or maybe that's the other way around. At any rate, Chalis"—the soft sound of his special pronunciation fell like a benediction on her ears—"before we talk, I think you need a warm bath and a cold meal. I'll handle one or the other—or both. It's up to you."

She swallowed, only then realizing that her lips had been parted ever since she had gotten herself ensnared in his hypnotic spell. "The kitchen's that way," she indicated vaguely, never once breaking contact with his penetrating gaze. Her brain finally shifted out of neutral and began to pick up speed, revealing a flickering succession of fascinating ideas.

"And the bath?" he queried with a tantalizing lift of one brow.

"I always wanted to be able to do that," she murmured abstractedly, and Benjamin's other brow shot up alarmingly.

"Most of us learn at an earlier age, but if you'll supply the soap and water, I'll be only too glad to provide the expertise."

"Soap and— No, I meant the eyebrow thing." A tiny smile was seeded and grew into a wide beam. She wriggled her nicely arched brows expressively. "I can manage the bath alone, thanks, but the cupboard's awfully bare. If you're really hungry . . ." Her voice trailed off as she made a reluctant move toward the bedroom.

"Trust me. If all else fails, we can send out."

Shaking herself out of the powerful spell of his nearness, Chalis escaped to her room and yanked open her closet as she began peeling off her clothes.

Her eyes lit on a white silk jersey tube which was particularly flattering, but she decided against it. It was entirely too blatant.

Jeans and sweat shirt? No, that wasn't right, either. Darn it, if she had any idea of what was on Benjamin's mind, she might know what to wear! She'd feel an utter fool if she draped herself in something seductive and he settled down over ham sandwiches and launched into a "Davie County Home-Farm Hour."

On the other hand . . .

She left it for the moment and ran the tub full of lukewarm water, throwing in copious handfuls of heliotrope bath salts. She'd probably slip and break her neck climbing out—which might solve her dilemma!

Absentmindedly submerging, she came up and shook her head in irritation. Two minutes with Benjamin and she reverted to Quarter Moon bathing habits! As she removed the suds from her eyes, questions began to rise to the surface of her mind. First and foremost, what was he doing here? Could it be connected with Lara and the gallery? Could it be her uncle?

Uncle Leonard! That was it! No wonder he had persisted in trying to reach her. No wonder he'd been staring at her with that soft-eyed look that fused all her brain circuits! He was trying to break it to her gently!

"Benjamin!" she yelled over the sound of the blender.

Pulling the drain plug, she opened her mouth to

yell again, and then her eyes widened as the door opened and Benjamin stuck his head inside the bathroom.

"Did you call me?"

"Of course I called you! Get out of here!" She scrabbled with one foot to shut off the drain, covering her breasts with her arms.

He moved just inside and leaned against the wall, looking dark and alien against the steamy pink-and-white tiles. "Gregory's been shorting you on rations, hasn't he? You'll never fatten up at that rate."

"I don't know what you're talking about," she grumbled, leaning against her updrawn knees to glare at him. "Kindly get out, and stop staring and hand me that towel!"

"As cool and logical as ever, I see." He knelt beside the tub and reached out one long, tanned forefinger to catch a slither of suds as it commenced a downhill slide over the slope of her breast.

Her voice caught somewhere in the back of her throat. "Benjamin—please don't start anything."

"You started it, Chalis, about fifteen years ago, give or take half a dozen." His hand moved easily under her slippery arm to find what it sought, and she lowered her eyes to watch the blatant betrayal of her body. Against a milk white cone, her nipple darkened excitedly as it thrust itself against his seeking hand. She lifted her gaze beseechingly to see the sudden flattening of the planes of his face as a flush mounted higher under his deep tan. "Chalis . . . God, how I've missed you!"

With an impatient exclamation, he stood and drew her to her feet, catching her as she slipped on the treacherous surface. His arms swung her up, oblivious to the wetness that quickly soaked his navy shirt, the pale gray pants, and he carried her through to the bedroom.

"Benjamin, this is no good," she demurred once, and he answered her protest with his lips, sealing off all resistance until it withered and died in the heat of a far more powerful emotion.

"It's good," he breathed against her mouth. "It's so good, sweetest heart."

"We were going to talk." Feeble last protest.

"Later," he promised as his free hand went to his belt.

They both froze at the sound of a rap on the outer door. Benjamin's glance questioned her, and then they heard the sound of a key in the lock. Only one person besides Chalis had a key. Tansey had used it to water the plants while she was gone. "Tansey?" Chalis murmured. Good Lord, she hadn't been joking about her curiosity, had she?

"Benjamin, you're about to meet your adoring public," Chalis informed him, amusement tempering the frustration that racked her. "Go on out there. I'll dress and come on out in a minute."

Resignedly, he stood up, straightening his clothes. "I've waited almost three weeks. Another thirty seconds won't kill me, I suppose, but don't bother to dress. In the words of a famous general and a French perfume, 'I shall return.'"

She giggled. And then the sound faded as Walt's voice came through the thin paneled door. "Chalis, are you here? Sorry to be so long, my dear, but traffic was unbelievable."

The look Benjamin leveled at her defied interpretation. She could only shake her head in rebuttal of the accusation she imagined she saw there.

Benjamin stepped through the door and closed it after him, and Chalis was off the bed before the last click of the latch sounded. Naked, she leaned against the cool painted surface and listened unashamedly. What on earth was Walt thinking of, using her key and talking as if he made a habit of it! He sounded like a harried husband, home from work! Whatever must Benjamin be thinking?

Whatever must *she* be thinking! Backing away, she wrapped her arms defensively around herself and stared at the reflection in the mirror. Good Lord, had she lost what feeble mind she possessed? After all her resolutions, all her rationalizations, the man had only to show up, and five minutes later she was in bed with him!

She had finally settled the question of her future, and it didn't include either of them. Not Walt—not Benjamin. She'd go on working for Walt if he'd let her, but as for Benjamin, he was only a childish infatuation she had long since left behind, a remnant of her safe, secure background, which still haunted her occasionally under the guise of homesickness.

And the means of her physical awakening, she reminded herself with a soft, defeated moan.

Scrambling in her drawer, she dug out a pair of white cotton trousers and a crocheted string pullover. She tugged them carelessly on over her still-damp body and raked a comb through her dripping hair. Chin lifted, she braced herself to throw open the bedroom door and set her house in order, once and for all. Job's were scarce, but they weren't impossible to find. And as for the other, where was the chance for happiness with a man who admittedly avoided any but the most casual relationships with his women? Her instincts had served her badly in the past, but this time, when they told her that she couldn't survive that sort of relationship with Benjamin, she had to trust them.

Throwing open the door, she exclaimed, "Both of you, listen here to me!" And then she blinked and peered around the empty room. "Walt? Benjamin?"

"Did you call me?" Benjamin appeared in the kitchen door, a calico mitt on his hand. "Spanish omelet"—he nodded to the cast-iron pan resting on the open door of the oven—"*más o menos.*"

"What happened?"

"Gregory? I sent him packing. Oh, don't worry, he's still intact, only he won't be barging into your apartment anymore." Reaching into his pocket, he brought out a single key on a small ring and tossed it into the air once before catching it and restoring it to its coveted place on his hip.

"But what did he want? Benjamin, Walt's never—I mean, he doesn't—"

"Seems his secretary told him you wanted to see him rather urgently, gave him the key. Any idea why?"

Chalis hooked one of the two kitchen chairs with her foot. She had forgotten to put on shoes, but that could wait. "That little devil! Tansey's had a thing about Walt ever since I've known her, but then, Tansey has a thing about at least four different men, up to and including Omar Sharif. I guess she thought she could bring certain matters to a head this way. I don't know why else she'd send him over here, knowing you were here."

Benjamin put the heavy frying pan on a hot pad on the table and tested the golden baked omelet. There were flecks of red and green on its surface and the aroma was tantalizing. "You serve the plates and I'll pour the coffee. I was going to make it cold cuts, or something on that line, but all I could find was half a dozen eggs and a few raw vegetables. No wonder you're wasting away."

Ignoring the disparaging comment, she tasted the omelet, discovered she was famished, and polished off two-thirds of her serving before she said, "Your domestic talents astound me, Mr. Poe."

With a patently false look of modesty, Benjamin claimed self-defense. "Pearl can be lethal over long periods. I had to learn to cook as a preventative measure."

"Why do you keep her on?" She helped herself to another slice, savoring both the impromptu supper and the easy way they could slip in and out of a comfortable camaraderie.

"She worked for my grandparents as a girl, and stayed on to keep house after they died. Jean and I were living in Bermuda Run, and instead of letting the house stand empty, I let Pearl live there in exchange for keeping it up. She loves the house, hates to cook. Always has. But I can't see hiring on a cook for just me."

Chalis poured herself another cup of coffee and topped off Benjamin's cup. "Why didn't you live there with Jean?" She was far beyond standing on ceremony at this point. If the question offended him, he could refuse to answer it.

His eyes focused on a copper fish mold hanging above the range. "Jean . . . well, let's just say Jean thought she knew what she wanted until she got it. Then she discovered that it wasn't all that desirable."

Chalis remained silent, willing him to continue. She didn't dare speculate on where her relationship with Benjamin was going, or if it would even get off the ground. But if it did, then she didn't want it shot down by either Jean or Lara. If there were any more women in his past, and there probably were, they could wait until she knew where she stood.

"Before we were married, Jean professed to *adore* fishing and riding and spending an occasional lazy day at the pond, just like she *adored* Yadkin Trace. Her words," he added with no discernible hint of bitterness. "After we were married, every time I wanted to spend an afternoon fly-fishing or riding the river trail, or just relaxing on a raft at the pond, her blasted *hair* had to be done! No sooner would we get started than she began to fidget, wondering if we were going to get back in time for her to shampoo her hair. The whole damned Middle East crisis would be held up while Jean messed about with her hair, if she had her way!"

Chalis, whose hair care involved showering and blow-drying, plus a monthly trim, smiled in commiseration. Her own hang-up was teeth. She was a nut about brushing and flossing.

"That's a petty thing to pick out, but I'm afraid it was typical of the thousands of petty things that split us up. As for living at the Trace, that didn't suit Jean, either. Her friends were all outdoing each other to see who could spend the most on a house, and she had to get into the game. I guess it just boiled down to incompatibility. We were both young, and I guess the attractive early plumage disguised the nature of the mature bird. I gave her the house in Bermuda Run, which she promptly sold, and now I think she's living somewhere near San Francisco."

Moving in concert, they put the dishes in the sink and Chalis ran hot sudsy water on them. She reached for her rubber gloves, but Benjamin caught her hand. "Let 'em wait. I haven't been hanging around this town for two days to watch you wash dishes."

"No, I don't suppose you have," Chalis murmured, aware of a hollowness in her chest now that the moment of truth was at hand. If she'd just made a fool of herself for the second time, she'd soon know it. "Benjamin . . . what are you doing here? I thought at first that it might have something to do with Lara, and then I was afraid—" She hesitated meaningfully. "Uncle Leonard?"

"Your uncle's fine. He sends his love. As for why I'm here, I may as well confess. I was going to give you a month, then I was coming after you. If I had to offer to sell out and move up here and find a job as a law clerk, I'd have done it." His eyes gleamed tauntingly as he added, "But to be perfectly frank, I hoped you'd feel my noble gesture was enough, without putting it to the test."

She hardly heard his words as she steeled herself to lay her cards on the table, to offer him as much or as little as he wanted, with no untidy strings to entangle him afterward. "Benjamin, I have a feeling you're about to make some sort of proposition, and before you do, I want you to know that whatever happens, I'd like us to still be friends."

When he failed to respond, she made herself look at him. Was it exasperation or disgust that had tightened his mouth like that? "Benjamin . . . ?"

"Didn't you hear a single thing I said, woman? What do you think I want with you? Your delectable body? Damned right, I do! Your stubborn, pigheaded, illogical mind? I'll take it! Your—"

"Benjamin, stop yelling at me! If this is a sample of your big seduction scene, then you can—"

"When I start my big seduction scene, you'll be the first to know! Meanwhile, will you kindly shut up and let me get through with this damned speech? I rehearsed it for three solid hours on the way here Wednesday morning!"

She sank back into the dark blue silk cushion, her finger tracing the petals of a pale lotus blossom as a light began kindling in her eyes, in her heart. "What about this law clerk thing? The law of the open range, you mean? The law west of the Pecos—or at least west of the Yadkin River?"

"I told you I took a couple of degrees. One of them happens to be law. I don't practice, but it helps to be able to speak the language when I'm involved in complicated business dealings."

"Business deals? What business—" She sat up and stared at him.

"Will you pipe down? Now, where was I? Oh, yes,

about taking you. Now, I know what I said about two kinds of women. I recall mentioning something about not trusting my instincts where women were concerned, too. Matter of fact, I had originally planned to throw out a lure, see if you'd pick it up, and then reel you in, enjoy a short fling while you were there, and then toss you back again, unharmed."

"You dastardly cad," she breathed softly. Her fingers curled into her palms in an effort to resist touching the lines that ran from his aquiline nose to the corners of his mouth.

"Then I seem to remember deciding to do you a favor by getting you off the hook with Gregory. He'd have made you miserable, honeylove."

"Walt. Honestly, Benjamin, I've told him a dozen times I couldn't marry him, but he's as stubborn as Clyde's mule. He still thinks I'll give in."

"No, he doesn't. I told him before he left Carolina that if he so much as touched you, I'd tan his hide and nail it to the side of the barn."

Her finger found its way to the seam that ran down the side of Benjamin's neatly fitted trousers. As she followed it with her fingernail, her eyes lingered hungrily on the powerful muscles of his thighs. Something warm and exciting was beginning to happen in the pit of her stomach, and she leaned closer and brushed her cheek against his shoulder.

"Do you reckon Lara would be offended if I said something of the kind to her? She likes wall hangings. She told me so."

"Honey, you don't have to worry about Lara. We've never been anything but strictly platonic. We ran across each other during a bad patch in both our lives. She's divorced and remarried the same man twice now, and in between, she likes variety. I like the woman. She's honest and she's a damned fine artist, but basically, I'm a monogamous creature and Lara is anything but. If you'll pardon the jargon, I prefer a one-on-one relationship."

"Is this the opening shot of your seduction?" she teased. By now her fingers had found the embossed brass buckle he wore and were absently searching for the combination.

"All right, all right, greedy-eyes! Go ahead and seduce me if you just can't wait, but I'm an old-fashioned fellow. You'll have to promise to make an honest man of me afterward!" He pounced on her then, and they both rolled off the silk cushions to the deep nap of the carpet. "Hey, did I tell you I love you?" he whispered as his hands worked on the drawstring of her pants. "I do, you know—to a mortifying, almost incapacitating degree. It's embarrassing in a man of my years."

Her hands stilled in their task of unbuttoning his shirt. "Oh, Benjamin, are you sure? I mean really, *honestly* sure? Because I love you so hard it's been tearing me apart. I tried to pretend it was only because I had known you back in the happy days with my family, that you were just a symbol of security for me, and because you were the first man to . . . well, you know."

"I should have married you back when you were nubile and manageable," he taunted, tossing aside her clothes and making a fingertip survey of her topography. "Lord knows how I'm going to handle a high-stepping career woman."

She finished unbuttoning his shirt and began working on the recalcitrant buckle again. "Oh, well. As that old philosopher Doris Day once said, '*Que será, será.*' "

Silhouette Desire

Coming Next Month

A Kiss Remembered by Erin St. Claire

Ten long years simply disappeared the moment Shelley Browning saw Grant Chapman again, but it was still a student/teacher relationship. Only this time Shelley wasn't concerned with breaking university rules.

Beyond Fantasy by Billie Douglass

Deanna Hunt had never known anything like the passion she had discovered with Mark. Hopelessly in love, she wondered if the architect who had shattered her perfect life would be there to pick up the pieces.

Chase The Clouds by Lindsay McKenna

Dany knew it was ludicrous to hope that a fiery stallion could ever compete as a Grand Prix jumper—but one look from the devastatingly handsome owner and all doubt was replaced by hope . . . to share in his impetuous dream.

Silhouette Desire

Coming Next Month

Summer Thunder by Elizabeth Lowell

High fashion model Holly North had her work cut out for her: to prove to cynical rancher Lincoln McKenzie that her beauty was more than skin deep, and that her love was worthy of his trust.

Stormy Serenade by Suzanne Michelle

Top photographer Kiki Andrews had returned to Texas to photograph country singing sensation Stoney Blue—not to fall in love with him. But now that she had met the perfect man, she wouldn't allow him to escape.

Blueprint For Rapture by Lenora Barber

Enraged that he'd unwittingly hired a woman contractor, Phelan Cannon attacked Gabrielle at first sight with both anger and desire . . . awakening in her a hunger that only he could satisfy.